WAKEFIELD STORIES

Wakefield Stories

John Casey

Contents

For Nicholas Fuhrmann, OSB

"His gift (disguised)"
Mark Burnett

I

Jim's Place-Iceledo, AR

When I recall the time I was cabin bound in a blizzard with that character Jim McReynolds and a couple of strangers, I start the memory with his phone call and suggestion that I drive up to his place to look at elk. I was pulling out of the Sonic on Greenwood Avenue in Fort Smith, my regular dining establishment since my divorce. I had their foot long chili cheese coney meal in my lap so I could get a head start on the tater tots when my phone rang. The screen said it was Jim. It had been a while. There was no one behind me so I stopped to take the call. Jim yelled in my ear, inviting me, in his formal fashion, to drive up and see the elk on his place. He's got forty acres next to Richland Creek Wilderness Area in Newton County, a twelve thousand acre tract so rugged the U.S. Forest Service released it from their logging inventory and let the environmentalists have it. Elk sometimes graze the little hay meadow below the bluffs which mark the edge of his property. He said there were a good number of them, maybe sixty cows, bedded down in the middle of the pasture. We yelled back and forth. I suspect he turns his TV up loud just before he calls just to annoy

3

me. Jim has a highly individualized sense of humor, you might say. When you live alone, I mean really alone, what seems comical can shift on you. "I can't promise they'll still be here but they were under the bluff yesterday. I'm keeping the dogs close. If you come up you might see them."

You can see elk in Boxley Valley about any time, but it had been a while since I had stayed with Jim in his cabin. His friends wonder if there's a more remote residence in Arkansas. I enjoy visiting his place; it's quiet and comfortable. His back porch overlooks a sloping hillside covered in grown up timber, hickories and black oaks, he tells visitors. Visitors are rare in winter. He can go four or five days, easy, without talking to anyone. This is unexpected, because Jim's a wit and a polymath. He can talk in an entertaining way about stuff that usually does not interest me, like motorcycles and military planes. He knows a lot about the origins of mankind. The first time he visited my house, when we were fifteen year old kids at boarding school, my mom took us to a dog show at the Civic Center. Jim knew the names of all the breeds and their histories. My mom, a dog lover herself, was charmed, and probably relieved that I had a friend who wasn't an idiot. Jim and I took to each other right away, many years ago now. What he saw in me I don't know. He was such a smart guy. I don't think I knew anything back then. In good weather we sat on Jim's porch and drank Scotch, and yakked about the old days. The invitation pleased me.

"What's the weather forecast?" I asked. I had heard that northern Missouri was getting clobbered by a south-moving blizzard, a storm you'd expect in North Dakota or Minnesota. Just as I asked, I lost concentration. A woman I know drove by right in front of me, her purse on the roof of her car. We taught together for years, before she retired because of health reasons. I had been thinking about her just the day before, it occurring to me that I couldn't remember the last time I saw her or thought about her. I liked her at one time and now I had kind of forgotten about her. This was the first in a string of unusual little events that happened around that time that I remember vividly--occurrences that I was part of but did not create.

There was nothing I could do about my friend and her purse. She went by me in a long line of cars. I watched her drive out of sight, not knowing that her driver's license, phone, money and credit cards, and maybe meds, were six inches above her head. It was frustrating to see her car vanish in traffic. I hoped the people behind her would try to get her to stop but they hadn't yet. It had been grey and dreary most of the week. I think weather changes people. Maybe folks weren't in the mood to look out for their fellow man. It doesn't take much for our better impulses to go away.

"Sorry, Mac, I got distracted. What did you say?"

"It'll be colder than a bear's ass. Lows in the teens. Highs in the twenties. The south edge of the big storm that's hitting Saint Louis might extend as far south as Harrison, probably tomorrow night. We'll dodge it at my place but if you come up tomorrow we'll drive to Harrison and stock up on groceries and whiskey before the roads get bad. Can you bring me a half dozen cigars? Macanudos, those Upmans you like, anything. I'll pay you."

It was the day before Christmas Break so I had time to burn but I didn't want to get up there and not be able to get out. As much as I like being in Iceledo, two or three nights is enough. It turned out Jim was right about the temps, but people all over North Arkansas ended up cussing the weather forecasters for the part they missed. Unlike a lot of people, I think weather forecasters are generally very good, but that week I joined the mob that condemned them.

The next morning I put one of those little oil-filled heaters that they sell at Yeagers, the ones that look like radiators, in the back seat of my truck before I left the house, along with a few clothes in a duffel. I included running shoes and cold weather running duds. Part of the reason I wanted to visit Iceledo was to start an exercise program, for the thousandth time. The timber roads are a good place to run. It's disgraceful how fat I'd gotten.

The extra clothes would come in handy in Jim's cabin. He wears a fleece inside all winter. I never met anybody who likes to suffer so much. I put out extra food for my old tom cat, Hector, and walked next door to ask my neighbor, Mrs. Meyers, to watch my place for me. She's met Jim and likes him, but she doesn't approve of him. Women have always been drawn to Jim, but sometimes in a maternal way, like he's a project to complete.

"One of these days you're going to go up there and find him dead." Like a lot of retired nurses, she talks plain. "Living up there like that."

"That's all right," I said. "I always take a shovel."

She shook her head. "Wait a minute. I've got something for you. Give half of these cinnamon rolls to Jim. I'll check on Hector. He'll be okay."

I was tempted to stick the full pan of cinnamon rolls in my freezer. I'd rather share money with a pal than Margaret Myers' cinnamon rolls, but I made myself set them on the passenger seat along with some CD's, Jim's copy of Pushkin's Eugene Onegin he lent me, which I was never going to finish, no matter how good he said it was, and a good sleeping bag. On the way out of town I bought a hundred dollar's worth of cigars at Winston's. We'd spend more than that at Bypass Liquors in Harrison. Disgraceful. To redeem myself I spent a few bucks buying bones for Jim's dogs at Paul's Meat Market.

The drive to Mac's place gets stimulating at the bottom of the escarpment north of Clarksville which separates the Arkansas River Valley from the Ozark Plateau. Our Ozarks aren't tall mountains but we can tell you that they are rugged. I always feel some state pride when I get to the mountain counties. Before that, as usual, I was like a robot on I-40. I couldn't tell you what I thought about. I can tell you where my mind was when I got on twisty Hwy 123, rising up steeply from the river valley, although it is a little embarrassing to admit that as I was driving too fast through the continuous curves. In my mind I was in a Lamborghini, zooming through the esses at LeMans, not a middle age track coach and math teacher in a four cylinder Toyota pickup. I can own up to this fantasy, unlike some others I wallow in regularly.

I made one stop on the way up. The Forest Service had the gate to Haw Creek Falls Campground locked, so I pulled a windbreaker over my fleece, ducked under the barrier and trotted down the lane to the campground. When you're hiking by yourself and the temps are below freezing, even a short hike has a seriousness about it. You feel it when you walk away from your vehicle. The trees along the lane stood in patient, motionless silence, as if they knew the temperature had dropped and were brooding in expectation. There was a spooky atmosphere around the empty picnic tables and vacant campsites. Nature was waiting for something. Damp woods on still winter days seem to have excellent acoustics for absorbing sound. The quiet was unsettling; I could hear my lungs fill and empty. As much as I love Haw Creek Falls, the cold and dreariness made me feel unwelcome and I knew that I would be punished if I used bad judgement or got careless. If I fell on the slick rock by the creek and cracked a bone or tore up a knee it would be a long limp to the car. I shivered as I paused on the flat slab rock near the falls. The water pouring over the lip was lively and had a nice jade tint—ice rimmed the edge in the quiet pool--but the sky was grey and menacing. I lay on my back on the slab rock and did leg lifts, then stared straight up as I rested. The woods were grey. The limestone I lay on was grey, as gray as the sky. It was as if I lay in a mausoleum.

I returned to some thoughts I had been having, thoughts about the state of my soul, wondering if I would ever become the person

I was supposed to be, the person I had always thought I would become. I know a few people who don't have evident flaws. Maybe I'm full of myself, but I think I had always assumed that I would someday be like them. The accusations I listened to at the end of my marriage weren't always fair or accurate, but some were—sufficient to chip away at the ideal version I had of myself. At forty, I was learning to live with the real me. Not that I'm a bad guy, but I need to be better. Realistically, at my age, would it happen? I started to doubt it. The thought made me feel fearful. Every day at school I walk past posters in hallways and classrooms which urge us to be the best we can be. They don't do much for me. They never say how damned hard it is to correct even our harmless flaws and bad habits. I'm suspicious that I have flaws I'm not aware of, defects that are obvious to those who know me. If I was honest, the odds weren't good I would ever rise above myself if I hadn't done it by now. It appeared to me that because of my weaknesses, I was doomed to be just another mediocre, lukewarm human, trudging through life. It was an ugly, joyless realization which made me feel powerless. Like the slab rock I lay on, the world at that moment seemed like a hard, uncomfortable place.

I sat up and stared at the pool beneath the ledge, pondering how long I could last in it and what my final moments would be like, questions old kayakers and canoeists like me sometimes ask themselves. Eventually my fingers started to ache from the cold, which released me from my morbid brooding. I broke from the spell of the creek when my back was turned, heading back down the lane, trotting or walking briskly around the ice filled potholes. My heart lifted a bit when my little truck, a refuge with heat and food and music, came into view.

An hour later I was nearing Jim's place. Deep in the wildest part of the state, Jim likes to tell people, "I live so far back when I get my mail it has owl shit on it." A mile or so out, I slowed as I passed the mailboxes of his two nearest neighbors. The first lane led to the hidden, custom built home of a retired naval captain and his wife. Jim was friendly with them on an occasional basis. He said they were well-educated and gracious. He said the husband had a certain command presence you would expect, given his profession. The second home was a shack right on the road in the middle of a debris field which spilled into the ditch. The most common items around the shack, which has a carpet of discarded items instead of a lawn, were old, rusted riding lawnmowers. There must have been a couple dozen of them. Jim says the old man who lives there, his neighbor for years, has never made eye contact with him. He is uncertain of the old man's real name. Their mail deliverer says he uses several aliases and has supported himself by filing insurance claims when his homes burn. There's not much middle ground in Newton County. But, at least you know where they stand. If a guy has Tibetan prayer flags on his porch or a Confederate flag covering his living room window, you know a lot about him just by driving past his place.

Jim's dogs greeted me when I drove down his lane, running alongside and baying at my truck with wild joy, canine joy, which is in a special category of happiness. After I petted them I cuffed them down and told them I'd have a bone for them later that night when we sat by the wood stove. I think Jim's dogs—Petie, the tough little fox terrier who takes after Jim, and Benny, the sweet mutt—miss seeing people. Not too sure about Jim. It had been several days since the dogs had seen anyone but their owner. Their happy fit soon passed. They got bored and circled my truck, sniffing the tires as I unloaded.

I had my things out of the truck before Jim opened his door. He descended the steps in a slow, twisting motion, wincing as both feet rested on each tread. He had on khaki pants and a blue sweat shirt over a collared shirt, dressy for him. It meant we were going to town. Cold as it was, he was wearing Teva sandals and socks, as always.

"Your knee is giving you hell, isn't it?" I said. "Or is it the stenosis?"

"Misery," he agreed, but he smiled as he gripped my hand. "My back is fine. It's this damned knee. Good to see you, Ed. Glad you came up." He asked me about the drive up. I told him how pretty Haw Creek Falls looked. I didn't tell him about my glum thoughts.

"I have to tell you there's a revised forecast. Harrison will get snow early this evening, a lot of it. We might get a dusting here after midnight. If we're going to go, we better go now. I know you just got out of the truck. Sorry." I peed in his front yard. You can't do that on Clifton Court in Fort Smith. "Let me stretch a minute," I said over my shoulder. "Should we bring cigars?"

"You bet."

"And a flask?"

"Excellent suggestion," he said. "We'll have a snort on the way back when we get off pavement."

"Should we bring the dogs?"

He thought about it. "Naw, we'll leave them. They haven't been out much today. They might think I'm taking them back to the shelter."

"They probably don't think too much of Harrison," I said. Jim started to say something but just shook his head.

I stood in the doorway to his little home and inhaled. In my book the smell of a roast cooking rivals a touch of perfume on a nice woman's throat, the test of a realist over a romantic. Jim's place looked good. His furniture is of good quality, but just a sofa and a couple of upholstered chairs and a coffee table in the living room flanked his wood stove—a squat, Nordic looking cast iron box which sits on a rock apron. The rest of the floor is pine one-by-four, pretty scuffed. He's a neatnik, but dog hair has become part of the décor. His cabin is contemporary with a vaulted ceiling, tall windows, and flat white sheetrock walls which keep the place from being too dark, the structure contractor-built under trees which grow next to the house on three sides.

The walls were framed with two by sixes, well stuffed with insulation. He could keep the little place warm if he wanted. A big Tim Ernst photo and a portrait of his late father and a cryptic quote by Stephen Crane, nicely matted and framed, hang at eye level on one wall. My favorite wall piece is a big map of Arkansas with the geographic regions color outlined, covering most of the opposite wall next to the screen door which leads to the porch. You can walk between the back of his couch and a breakfast counter which divides the kitchen from the living room. A short hall leads to the bathroom and a laundry room. Above the tiny kitchen is an open loft, reached by a set of stairs which right turns, starting at a landing behind the open door. A ceiling fan circles in his loft day and night. The bed is not spacious but Jim claims he has seen shooting stars through his skylight which he could touch if he stood on his bed.

He owns just a few dress shirts and pants, mostly corduroys and khakis. They hang on a rack as he has no closet. His guns—he has several—are hidden somewhere. His place is always clean, with the impression that every object is placed with precision. There's not so much as a nail head sticking up or a spot needing a paint touch-up in the house. I turn his toilet paper roll around every time before I leave.

"Jim, what's this bed doing downstairs?"

"It's this damned knee."

I could tell he didn't want to talk about it but I had to say something. "You're too young for this," I said. I drove out of the lot, as usual, in his vehicle—a nice, newer, four wheel drive Jeep Wagoneer, cherry red under a layer of Newton County dust turned to mud. White leather interior, CD's all over the dash. Jim talked with energy. I would have, too, if I hadn't talked to anyone in days. My end of the conversation may not have been brilliant, but I like to think that I do better than Petie and Bennie. He kept up a commentary on the land, game sightings and such. We yakked about the weather. Not everyone knows the difference between stratocumulus and cirrus clouds. I don't, and if I did, I would sound like a know-it-all if I expounded on it, but not Jim, which he did. I smiled when he said, "Newton County still does not have a stop light," satisfaction in his voice, when we passed through Jasper. He was more conflicted about the county's backwardness than he let on. I wonder if he knew it.

It was oppressively dark when we reached Harrison at four o'clock. We hurried to get our groceries. People shopped briskly for food items inside Harps. They were "stocking up" for the storm, more than one person said, but we were amused to see that the mood in the crowded aisles at Bypass Liquors was downright festive. Harrison ordinarily isn't a particularly friendly town, but jovial folks hailed us as they loaded cases of beer and wine into their carts. In line, people were talking about their generators.

"I got mine after that last ice storm," a man was saying. He kept repeating, "Never again."

"They won't have to go to work tomorrow," Jim muttered. "You know what that means to an imbiber." Not that I should judge. I licked my chops when Jim carefully set a fifth of 15 year old Dalwhinnie Scotch in our basket. $59.95! That wasn't all.

Jim and I are judgmental to the point of cruelty when we stereotype country people in general and people from Harrison in particular. The difference is that Jim's voice carries. He's the nicest, politest guy, but I sometimes have to worry about getting beat up when I am with him. We chatted in line with a nice looking woman who might have been about our age. She went on about her steep driveway. She could make this ordinary story interesting, being pretty and vivacious. I mentioned her looks as we walked to the car. Folks were walking by. Jim agreed, then said her last stop before going home would be at the dry cleaners to pick up her husband's Klan robes, a snarl in his voice. I looked around to see who heard. I noticed he got a sideways look from a guy behind us.

Flakes were starting to settle on the pavement. There was no urgency in their descent. They rocked as they fell, but they fell vertically in the still air. They vanished when they hit the asphalt, but the ugly yellow tint of the sodium street lights made the little landscape islands in the parking lot look like the stiff winter grass was covered in ash. The air was thick with the flakes, always a pretty and exciting sight when you haven't seen snow in a while, but I felt an urge to get out of town, thinking then that we were a bit ahead of the storm, not already under it, as I would learn later. As much as I did not want to spend the night in a car buried in a snowdrift or in a ratty Newton County forty dollar a night hotel, my traveling companion was unconcerned, as usual, and maybe secretly eager to embrace the experience, with its prospect of discomfort and maybe a dash of misery. "A benign snow," Jim said. "Hosts floating down from heaven. Your sins are forgiven, Ed, numerous as they are." He was the most Catholic non-Catholic I ever knew.

I drove way too fast getting out of Harrison. Traffic was light so I made good time getting to the outskirts, where I picked up the speed even more on the wet pavement, making good time down Hwy 7 for several miles, until the flakes started to stick on the road. The grass along the roadside was no longer visible.

Staying on the pavement was becoming a challenge. The visibility got so bad that it would have been hazardous to drive fast even if the snow hadn't stuck to the pavement. Jim was delighted, talkative as he leaned forward, his hands on the dash, helping me navigate the curves. Wind gusts rocked the Cherokee. I would have loved it too if I had known we would make it home. We passed cars in the ditches, and I was relieved that they were empty and we could drive on. I was like those selfish people I had mocked who were following my friend with her purse on the roof of her car.

"Do you remember when our canoe and all our gear took off down the White River without us?" I asked Jim.

"Sure," he said.

"Do you remember the first thing my wife asked me when she heard about it?"

"Yep, she said, 'Was alcohol involved?'"

"And it was," I said. "Did we go to Harrison for groceries or for whiskey? Just asking."

He laughed. "Pull over when we get to the square in Jasper. We'll cut a glass of Dalwhinnie with a bit of snow. We'll see what we run out of first."

We crept through Jasper on four inches of snow. It was coming down like it was shaken out of a sack. The windshield wipers worked to sweep the snow off the glass. Jim thought it was dry stuff, predicting drifts at the top of the mountain. At the bottom of the mountain the blue lights of a state police car illuminated a semi, helpless on its side, like an ox. We hoped the semi driver was sitting in the squad car. "I wish we could stop and give the poor son of a bitch a drink," Jim said, but the drive up the mountain from Jasper is one of the longest and steepest grades in the state, so I went by the police car as fast as I could, knowing success meant keeping my speed up. The cop was hardly going to chase me down and ticket me. We made it, thanks to four wheel drive and the fact that we were driving on a thousand dollar's worth of tires. Anyone coming up the mountain an hour later would have a hard time of it. I will say that Jim complimented my driving, which pleased me. He said, "Ed, you're driving like Tazio Nuvolare." Men, who have more wrecks than women, love to think that they are good drivers. My last ex was an excellent driver. I often told her so, until one day I realized that her skill behind the wheel meant little to her, or any other woman I have known. I mentioned this to Jim. "Women are inscrutable," he said.

So I was proud and relieved when we made it to the top. We stopped at the windy overlook and poured that drink. We got out, where I peed, quickly, while Jim stood by the rock wall, staring into the abyss. At the end of the parking lot the snow drifted almost waist deep against the rock wall. I was shocked. Was I still in Arkansas? We were yelling and laughing. I was young and giddy again. If Jim had been the right woman, I would have asked her to dance. He left his door open. The stereo was audible; I laughed, thinking it was an improbable place to listen to Delta Blues. I was drinking whiskey with Jim McReynolds in a blizzard, listening to Lightnin' Hopkins, the wind blowing a gale. It was stimulating, but before long my face and hands started to feel raw. When we got back in the car Jim said, "I'm going to fall on that roast like a saber-toothed tiger."

We thought we were near Cowell—we couldn't tell—and close to the community of Lurton and the network of roads through Ozark National Forest which would lead us to Jim's place when he yelled for me to stop. He said, "You're going off the road!"

We were entering a curve on a crest. I was going about twenty miles an hour, following the nearly filled in tracks of previous vehicles, when Jim barked his warning. I tapped the brakes a tad hard, which caused us to fishtail a bit, but we stopped on the level so at first I thought he was wrong. Between sweeps of the wipers I could see someone had spun around in the snow before they drove off the road. It was hard to be sure, but it did look like that while the road went straight the ruts followed the arc of the curve out of the cone of the headlight. Sure enough, I might have followed them down into the ditch. Jim lifted his cup full of whiskey to his mouth for a big draft then set the cup on the console between us.

"I better look," he said as he slid off his seat. He left the door open again. Cold air blew flakes in the car. I watched him in the head-lights, pacing in front of the Jeep, head down, the snow swirling around him. When I think about him, my memory has selected this moment to return to among thousands of others. It was like looking at a movie scene. There was something fascinating about it. Owing to his spine problems and a bad knee, he walked crab-like around the ruts, lifting his sandaled feet out of the snow, indifferent to the cold. The snow landed in his white hair and on his shoulders. He walked to the edge of the road. I felt a slight suspicion that he was up to something. There would be a diversion from our trip home. I pulled alongside him. "Someone's in the ditch," he said. "I can see headlights. They were coming toward us, lost control, and went off the opposite side of the road."

I had to leave the car in the lane so I turned the flashers on and left the passenger door open before I followed Jim down the slope. It wasn't too steep but it was a ways to the bottom, maybe forty yards before the swerve marks in the snow ran out to level ground. I wouldn't have wanted to be in that car during the sled ride down the hill. It was very dark, and danged hard to see. I prayed the car would be upright. It was upright and it was on level ground, the motor running. We approached through its headlights. The driver's side window dropped four inches. "Can you help us?" A female voice, faint.

Jim had his nose down by the window while I stood by the back door. The interior was not visible. I hoped there weren't kids in there.

"Ma'am, we'll do what we can," Jim was saying to the opening to the window. "Are you all right?"

I couldn't hear her clearly, but Jim said, "People pick worse places in Newton County to go off the road. I'm glad you're okay. What can we do?" I had a pretty good idea of what she wanted.

Jim hesitated. "No. I'm sorry, but only a wrecker can get this car back up that hill."

I walked around the vehicle. It was an Impala, a nice car, and it looked like it survived the sled ride. I heard Jim say, "I can do that. I have service at my house and I'll be glad to make calls for you. If I make it home. I can call the state police and tell them where you are and I can call a wrecker for you and I can call a family member for you, but you better let me make a couple of suggestions. Can we get in?" She took too long. I thought, "Hell, lady, I know we're strangers, but we're trying to help you, and I'm freezing my ass off in this wind." I was wondering if she lived locally. A husband in a four wheel drive could come get her. Or, if we had to, we could give her a ride home but how long would that take? Jim said, "Let's get in, Ed." The door was unlocked. He followed me in. The dome light was on. I pushed stuff out of the way, plopped on the seat. Working at Northside, I'm used to minorities, but it was a bit of a shock to be in the car with two black women. If Jim was taken aback he hid it. He introduced us with a formal politeness, calling the gals "ladies." The driver said her name was Gloria Johnson. She said she was pleased to meet us. She looked to be about our age, but I grew to suspect that she was older. She had a nice sweet face, with round features. The passenger had that Egyptian look some women have, high cheekbones and small chin, thin neck. She was regal looking. She had short, straight hair that lay close to her head. She said, "I'm Ella," as chilly as the air outside. They were trying to disguise it, but those women were rattled. They had slid off the road, their car probably spinning around a couple of times as it went down a hillside. They were in a blizzard in Newton County, had no cell phone service, and now had two strangers in their car, a couple of honkies with liquor on their breath. I didn't have to wonder if they lived locally anymore. You'll see an ivory billed woodpecker before you'll find a black person living in Newton County. "Okay," Jim said. "How much fuel do you have?"

"Over half a tank," Gloria said. "We filled up in Little Rock. More than enough to get us to Harrison, I thought. We have a meeting there tomorrow morning, at the courthouse."

"We can call a wrecker, but we won't be able to call you and tell if one will come tonight. I would bet that one won't. As much as we'd like to, we won't be able to come back and check on you. I'm not sure we can get home. I won't have cell phone service till I get to the top of the mountain where I live."

"What should we do?"

"I think your choices are to stay in your car or come with us. If you stay, you have enough fuel to stay warm for several hours if you're careful. You'll probably be safe. Most people around here are nice, not that I think you'll see any of them. Highway 7 is closed. I don't know when it will open. This is an unusually bad storm. What you need to think about is tomorrow. I think you'd end up walking to a house after you run out of gas."

"You can't drop us off at a hotel?"

"Ma'am, there are none. This end of the county has no amenities. There is a hotel in Jasper, but it's probably full, and if we try to get down that mountain we'll end up off the road, too.

Gloria stared through the windshield. "Well, I'm sure our meeting is canceled. I don't know what to do."

I interrupted. "Ladies, I don't want to make things more difficult for you, but you need to decide very soon," I said.

It was quiet for a moment. "May I ask the nature of your business in Harrison?" Jim asked.

"I work for the social security administration in Little Rock. I have to meet with the staff in the Harrison field office."

"I'm a retired hearing officer with the agency myself," Jim said. "I met with clients in that office many times. Drove up from Little Rock regularly. It's how I found my current home.

"Well, I'll swear," Gloria said.

"John Beasley was my supervisor. We retired about the same time."

"I knew him! I knew John. When I came on…"

"Guys! We have to go," I said. "You don't need to stay in this car. Jim has a nice place, plenty of room. We got a roast in a crock pot waiting. We're not bad men. Tell us what you want to do."

They didn't have the shoes for trudging up a hillside covered in a foot of snow, carrying luggage, and they wore short jackets, designed for keeping them warm when they walked from their car to a store on a brisk day. Thank goodness they had hats and gloves. Gloria staggered up the hill, clutching some files in a big envelope to her chest. She fell to her knees once. Jim helped her up. It's hard to get up when your arms are full. I could tell Jim was in pain, but he kept encouraging her. He had spinal stenosis and a swollen knee, and he was carrying a laptop and a purse, folding clothes, and a suitcase designed for rolling through airports. I asked him how he was doing. He ignored my question, but he leaned to me and said, "What if they're Baptists and won't let us drink?"

I hadn't thought of that," I said in a low voice. I looked over my shoulder. "Let's ditch 'em," I said. "It ain't too late."

Ella got halfway up the hill and realized she didn't have her phone charger. I was winded, glad to wait for her. It was farther to the top than I thought. I'm not fascinated by cars like Jim, but I never loved one more than when I slid behind the wheel of the Cherokee. At that point I don't think our guests were nervous, just grateful and relieved to be out of the storm. I ejected the CD right away. I couldn't imagine those gals liking Delta Blues any more than the people in the liquor store in Harrison would, and it would have been excruciating to listen to Lightnin' Hopkins singing about saddling up his black mare with them in the back seat. The car warmed up quick and pretty soon we were on our way.

I shouldn't have been too surprised that I ended up in a car in a blizzard with two strangers, minority women, on my way to being cabin bound. Things happened to Jim, odd things that did not happen to other people, and these things in turn happened to you if you were with him.

For a spell the driving was easy, and, though I hesitate to use the word, enchanting. The ground was covered to a depth of about ten inches, was our guess. The trees were already bent over with snow, narrowing the road in places. Flakes were coming down thick and fast, mixed with sleety looking bits of ice that bounced off the hood. Wind gusts picked up powdery snow which had already fallen, mixing it with the stuff coming down. When I got my speed up to a certain narrow range, the Cherokee's big new tires rode on the snow. The ride was quiet and smooth like a sleigh. Usually, U.S. Forest Service road beat the hell out of vehicles. You can't keep a coffee cup on the dash. We didn't have sleigh bells, but Jim had a Mozart flute sonata floating out of the speakers. We were warm and getting close to home. I wanted to bust out the Dalwhinnie and drive faster, but after what they'd been through, those women were going to get mighty upset if I went too fast and fishtailed. The drink in my lap would count for more than circumstantial evidence in the trial that would immediately begin. I was mindful that we still faced a hurdle, a challenge that was getting worse by the hour. The last mile to Jim's place is poorly designed. You drop like a kestrel down to Iceledo Gap, a low spot in the mountains and the site of a long-gone community, then ascend steeply to the top of the next mountain where the lane to Jim's place intersects with the Forest Service road. Even when conditions are good it helps to get your speed up to get to the top. If you slide off the road, your vehicle will roll over and over down the mountain until a post oak or a hickory stops it.

Jim unbuckled his seat belt and turned around in his seat, unconcerned, chattering with Gloria about work. Gloria had made an assessment. She appeared to think that we were all-right guys. She chattered too, in a voice that was musical but a little dramatic, as unconcerned about being in the car with us as if a co-worker was giving a her a ride home in Little Rock traffic. Ella was quiet, her face set. She couldn't have been happy. I stole an approving glance at her in the rear view mirror. If you put one of those jeweled, cone-shaped hats on her she'd be perfect for a part in a movie about the pharaohs.

Everyone was happy when I was traveling about twenty miles an hour through the curves on level ground, but when we dropped off the top of the hill, the nose of the vehicle pointed down, and I started stab breaking, a technique school bus drivers are taught, it got quiet, tense quiet. It looked like we were flying down a white tunnel. I was scared. "Guys, we're good," I said, a lie. "I've got to keep my speed up." I did that and more. The Cherokee picked up speed despite my breaking. It was starting to slide sideways when I braked so I gave up just as we swooped across the low spot at the Gap. We raced uphill at first but soon lost momentum and speed. It was just too steep. I gave the motor too much gas and we fishtailed wildly from one side of the road to the other, the rear of the Cherokee swinging over to the uphill side of the road, then across the road to where the rear tires must have been close to the edge of the mountain. Jim got tossed around, the girls were saying, "Oh! Oh!" as I slapped the steering wheel in one direction then the next, over-correcting. We finally got centered in the lane, traveling pretty much straight ahead, but had slowed considerably and I knew we were not going to make it to the top of the mountain. The tires spun in the snow until we slowed to a halt. Then we started to slide backward and sideways. It was a sickening feeling, worse than the fishtailing. I don't know what stopped us before we hit the edge. I unclenched my fists from the steering wheel and settled back against the seat, reveling in that wonderful emotion, relief from fear.

"Eventful day, huh Ed?" Mac said.

We left the car parked in the road again. I didn't like it. A vehicle coming down the hill would fly into it or go over the edge. Someone could get killed. Tazio Nuvolare could not have driven that car backwards down the mountain to the level place at the gap. It would have to stay where it stopped until the snow melted off the road. The gals were game about having to walk again but I know they dreaded it. They agreed to leave everything except one bag, stuffed with things they'd need that night. We promised them that we'd walk back and fetch more of their stuff in the morning. We trudged up that mountain road single-file, like mountaineers up an ice field, following Jim who broke trail. I was glad he knew the road. It was dark and the air was so thick with swirling flakes that we could have gotten lost if we hadn't been on a road, could have strayed off the road like Gloria's Impala. It was a lot farther than the walk from their car to the Cherokee. I started to sweat and the cold wind penetrated my fleece. I take cold pretty well so I knew the gals had to be miserable. We got to the top and turned into the lane. Jim turned around. "Three hundred yards to the house, ladies. No more uphill," he said. By the time we reached the cabin my nose was running but I could not feel my upper lip.

I fed bolts into the cold stove while Jim showed the gals his bedroom upstairs and the bathroom with the view. An hour later the cabin was the scene of a quiet little celebration. It took that long for the little wood stove to glow. The women sat on the couch under blankets; each had a glass of red wine in her hand. I think they were too worn out to be uneasy about where they were and what had happened to them. Petie sat between them, staring at Gloria, desperate for her affection. She had coaxed him there, after securing Jim's permission, scratching his thick little skull with her long fingernails. The roast beef smelled wonderful. Jim offered to bring the plates to the couch but Gloria insisted that we sit at the table and was firm that we say a blessing. In it she thanked God for his divine assistance in sending us to help her and Ella. She was earnest and genuine and sincere, still, her prayer sounded like blasphemy to me, such that I had to suppress a grin. We concentrated on the meal, not saying much to each other. I asked Jim how he liked the meal. "I'm going to weep," he said, as he buttered a slice of his homemade bread. In disgust, I thought about Sonic.

The scariest part of winter outdoor recreation is the drive home. After being in the cold for hours your core temperature drops. You get in your car, warm up in little time, and think you are recovered, but it is almost predictable that you will fight a battle with a narcotic-like drowsiness. Many a hiker or kayaker I know has a story about being suddenly jostled awake, in a panic, having run off the road at dusk in heavy Interstate 40 traffic after a cold day paddling a creek or hiking a trail. So was with us. Lethargy set in right after the meal. I felt like an old bear that needed to hibernate. The gals and I tried to small talk while Jim put up the leftovers, but it was forced. Suddenly the cabin seemed too hot. We were listening to Lou Rawls, who has the warmest voice in popular music. His love songs worked like a lullaby on me. Male pride alone kept my chin from dropping. Finally, someone apologized and surrendered. The rest of us admitted we were helpless too, so we left the dregs in the glasses and went to our beds.

Jim snored, one of the gals snored and Petie snored in the winged back chair by the couch where I lay. I am a light sleeper but I was comfortable in the sleeping bag. I noticed the stove wasn't turning out much heat when I got up to use the bathroom the first time, so as quietly as I could, I fed the stove. I went to the window.

The snow still swirled down. The second time I used the bathroom I noticed girlie underthings drying on the shower curtain rod. The brassiere was a wrap, almost without cup. Ella. As I padded past Jim's bed in the hall he whimpered. Pain. I felt bad for him. I knew that there was more of that in store for him.

Hauling the girl's luggage up the mountain the next morning was a chore, but carrying the food, especially the twenty pound sacks of dog food, was misery. It took us two trips and we didn't get it all. It was the first time I ever walked through deep snow carrying sacks of groceries and the last I hope. Jim said Sherpas would balk at what we had to do. We wished we had a sled to pull. We wished we had packs on the dogs, who ran alongside us joyously. The snow was too deep for Petie but he didn't know it. It was cold—the thermometer on Jim's porch read seventeen degrees--but the stiff wind had died down before sunrise. Our last task was to write a warning note on a cardboard box which said the road was blocked by a vehicle half way down the mountain. We set the box in the middle of the road and piled some snow in it.

It gave us a chance to talk. "My plan is to phone the highway department and find out when Highway 7 will be bladed and open, then schedule a wrecker to pull the Impala up the hill to the pavement. I also need to contact the county to see when my road will be bladed. Other than watch the weather forecast, that's all we can do." I asked him how long he thought we'd be isolated. He raised his shoulders and shrugged. After the big ice storm in '08 he couldn't get off his property for a week. Fallen trees were all over the forest roads. He couldn't even get his vehicle down his driveway. At that time the cabin was unfinished, not fully stocked and used only on occasional weekends. He says he ran low on food and firewood. I suspect he ran plumb out of food and firewood, but when he spoke of it, he didn't seem to mind. A week would run us through Christmas. There was nothing else we could do. It was like going back in time, accepting what Nature gave us.

I said, "This could be tough."

Jim dismissed this with a wave. He had been through worse. He smiled and said, "I realize that this is a lot to ask, but if you sense that there will be an impending, high decibel intestinal eructation, from any exit, you might step away from the cabin." That was the extent of his anxiety.

"You're worried about me? You'll be in the cold all day," I said, but I wasn't feeling lighthearted.

He was still happy about the breakfast. Gloria had started fussing around the kitchen while it was still dark. Sweet woman that she was, she brought me a cup of coffee while I was still in my sleeping bag. When she turned her back I hopped out, got into some jeans and took my place at the table. Jim helped her in the kitchen. They yakked and yakked. He had found someone who liked to talk about food as much as he did. I believe he sent her a nice apron from Williams and Sonoma sometime later. Having Gloria around was clearly fine by him, but I figured if she didn't get to Little Rock in a day or two to shop for gifts and finish decorating for Christmas, nice as she was, she might be a terror to be around, but Jim always disregarded risk. Anyway she served up a breakfast of eggs, bacon, biscuits, gravy, and pancakes that was celestial. It was a rare treat for me. I usually start my day supervising cross country practice with a Starbucks coffee and pastry. After we destroyed the breakfast, we sat at the table for at least an hour, drinking coffee. Gloria had on pleated navy pants and a rose-colored fleece-like top that looked expensive and comfortable. Her features were nice and they conveyed kindness and decency. It had been a while since a woman had sat across a breakfast table from me. It had been even longer since a smiling woman sat across a breakfast table from me. Jim's cabin makes a statement: masculinity. Having Gloria at the table was a counter statement. She was a real woman, not a ghost we talked about. I enjoyed listening to them discuss work. Like most teachers and coaches, all I have even known is the school business. It looked like Gloria was brought in to Jim's old office from another unit so she could straighten out problems. Sweet as she was, I sensed that she could be tough. Some of the stories they told about clients who were denied disability status were sad. I got the idea that the system worked well most of the time, but they said every once in a while a deserving person got turned down due to a peculiar ineligibility status, and sometimes someone not just undeserving but despicable got awarded a nice check, maybe for life.

I listened to those stories, shook my head and said to myself, The things that happen to people. When I think about that stay in Iceledo, I become bewildered, thinking that for many of us, our lives are a welter of stories that are so unexpected they seem unfinished and fragmented, somehow, even after we're gone. I don't have the words to explain it, but I know it's a troubling feeling. You can read a novel in a few hours. You watch a movie in three. You watch your friend's lives for decades. If you outlive them like I did Jim you go back to their story, sometimes for years, especially if you were close to them and if you were a character in their story. Thinking about it, it gets to you. My last ex was a writer who said there are only about a dozen plots in fiction. She said each story is a variation on one of the twelve, but there are an endless number of personalities. I believe in the whole history of the world there has only been one Jim B. McReynolds. There will not be another one. I could spend the rest of my life looking for another and not find anyone like him. I hate that old expression, "They broke the mold when old so and so died," but I think a mold breaks when everyone dies. When Jim passed away, I felt bad but I didn't cry. His death was expected, peaceful and surprisingly painless, but damned if I didn't bawl for a couple of minutes while I was mowing my front yard a few weeks later, snuffling and sobbing while I pushed the mower back and forth across my fifty foot lot.

I had known for some time that he would not live to be an old man. Three months before his death, I visited him in his assisted living facility in Bentonville. The door to his apartment was partially open. I stuck my face in the opening and said his name twice, pretty loud, before I went inside. He was sitting in a kitchen chair in his hallway, staring at the floor, wearing a t-shirt and a diaper. I got a chair from the kitchen and sat next to him. Dementia came with the Parkinson's, but this was the first time he didn't know me. He repeated my name but he couldn't make the connections. Something was worrying him. He was trying to ask someone for another chance. The frustration he was feeling looked like an agony. He couldn't finish his sentences. I filled up the awful silence by giving him the news on people we were acquainted with and I talked about my job but the Jim I knew was gone. I didn't stay long.

He gave me lots to think about, and as much to laugh about. I haven't stopped.

Jim made us BLT's for lunch. After, he somehow got the girls outside for shooting practice. Did I mention his ability to get me in odd situations? His brand new .45 was too big for them and they were tentative at first, but pretty soon they were blasting away. Gloria was not even close to accurate, but she cracked us all up by saying in a stage voice, "How you want it, dawg? Closed casket?" as she opened up on the aluminum pie plate Jim had tied to a branch. The noise was deafening in the cold dry air. I didn't shoot. I don't like guns, though I am a second amendment defender. The shooting practice gave me a chance to do something I wasn't able to do in the cabin, which was to stand back and give Ella a good long stare. I can defend it. She was too bundled up to call it ogling. Over the years I have grown to appreciate good china, though I don't buy it. At home I drink out of old jelly jars, but I can appreciate a beautifully set table. Maybe I'm lying to myself, but resting my eyes on Ella's classic face didn't seem much different than examining a pretty porcelain plate. I certainly wasn't thinking about pursuing her. It took me forever, but I have learned to recognize a lost cause early in the romance game. In fact, it appeared that Ella did not want to get to know me even casually. She avoided eye contact with me and spoke in a friendly fashion only when I asked her something. It seemed to me that she was a bit friendlier with Mac. She had put up a wall between us. I had a mild interest in getting to know her and did not think I had ulterior motives but I was rebuffed. I admit that it would have been awkward if we had hit it off like Jim and Gloria had. I can't say why, but one couple pairing up seemed okay, while if Ella and I had followed suit, the implications would have seemed indelicate. We were snow-bound in a cabin, not on a double date. So I didn't blame her. I did have a flash of resentment in mid-morning when my attempt at small talk with her went nowhere. I have known guys who think that pretty women have an obligation to pay attention to them. Weak fools, they get mad when women don't respond to them. So I was troubled for a few minutes. Was I stung by the rejection? Before long I declared myself innocent. I consoled myself by remembering that I could not remember ever feeling resentment when I was rejected. It was an odd place to go for comfort but it worked.

Ella was impressive to look at, and she seemed like a bright person. She was tall and she moved gracefully. She looked real nice out there in the snow. She looked vulnerable, pacing and hugging herself to stay warm, not so much when it was her turn to shoot. She squinted and flinched as she pulled the trigger on the handgun. You can't take your eyes off a good-looking woman with a hot .45 in her hand.

By cocktail hour, I concluded that it had been a good day, though a dark, damp, cold one. Too damned cold for a cigar on the porch.

That ate at me. We want what we can't have. We were cooped up but the hours passed. I trotted outside for more wood. The girls read and napped. When she wasn't napping upstairs in the warm loft, Gloria worked on her laptop. Ella texted on her phone. Jim read one of his expensive Shelby Foote books on the Civil War, not for the first time. The cabin was quiet as a chapel. Jim and the girls seemed content. I tried not to pace. I watched the clock for five o'clock. Many people are like me: they drink because they are bored. I put my little radiator heater in the bathroom so the girls could have a pre-dinner bath.

Jim kept his bird feeders full of sunflower seeds. He spread a line of seeds on his porch railing. The chickadees and juncos couldn't keep it a secret. At dusk the women and I went to his windows more than once to watch a row of cardinals lined up on the porch railing. Jim said they were the last birds to leave his feeders every evening. There were three colors outside—the white snow, the charcoal tree bark and the crimson cardinal feathers. The slate grey sky was the canvas. It wasn't lost on the girls, or me, either. Jim made another phone call just before dinner was served.

"Ladies, I know you're curious about what I learned," Jim said at the dinner table. We were passing around salad and mashed pota- toes. It was Jim's custom to sear a filet on both sides, then broil it for guests. We had done nothing all afternoon but we were hungry. "First I should say that I will hate to see you leave my house, and I do hope you will return. You will find Iceledo a different world in late Spring. The good news for you is this: the dispatcher at the state police headquarters predicts that Highway 7 will be open by the day after tomorrow, possibly by noon. She did say that the driving con- ditions will not be good till some sun hits the pavement. I called a wrecker service in Deer, a little community east of here. Gloria, he added your Impala to the list of vehicles he's going to get to as soon as the pavement is bladed. He knew where the car was and he said it would be an easy extraction. I don't know anything about him but he seemed friendly and helpful. I did not discuss his fee. I did think to ask him if he took credit cards. He does.

"Wonderful," Gloria said. "Jim, you've been so good."

"We can't thank you enough," Ella said, "but you said that's the good news. Is there bad?"

"I have to get you to the highway. I know the man who grades the roads up here. He's my most appreciated government employee. It is predicted that he'll pass by my place sometime Friday. So, three good things have to happen. That's a lot for up here. This is a hard-luck country. An early settler said that Arkansas was not part of the world our Savior died for. I think he was referring to Newton County. On top of this, there's a slight chance for freezing rain tonight. Still, I think your chances are good. Ella, can I fill your wine glass?"

"Please, yes." She paused. "We're enjoying our stay. That bath...the...view....It was like I was in a resort. You both have been so nice. And the food! There's no telling what would have happened to us if you hadn't come along. I'm grateful. It's just that I want to get home. It's Christmas."

Her voice sounded a little shaky. Jim's voice was soothing. "We'll get you out of here as soon as we can."

Gloria spoke. "I feel the same way. It is a blessing that you're such nice men. Maybe I shouldn't say this, but we were worried that you were racists and would hurt us."

"We were worried that you were fundamentalists and wouldn't let us drink," I said.

"Not that the two are equivalent," Jim added.

Pretty close, if you factor in the cigars untouched in his humidor, I wanted to say, but I kept my mouth shut.

"I need to clear out of here too," I said. "I'll follow you down Highway 7 as far as Pelsor. If you come back up, please include me."

"This has been good for us," Jim said. "We've cut way back on our cursing. You are a civilizing influence!"

"You bet," I said.

"Jim, I can't believe you curse! You talk so pretty!" At breakfast Jim had told her that her pancakes would please the palate of a jaded epicure. Phrases like that rolled out of his mouth all day long. About all I could do was say, "Dang these pancakes are good." The man could curse, though, better than anyone I ever heard, a consequence of innate talent and lots of practice.

"Ed, you don't curse, do you?"

"Yes, ma'am. I'm foul. I don't like it. It's one of the harder habits to break. Don't start."

"Oh, I won't," she said.

We told our stories, confining them to school and work with a little stiffness in the deliveries. I guess it was too soon and too hard for us. I liked those women but there was a gulf between us. To my surprise, Gloria said she grew up in the country. Her father farmed a little place a thirty minute school bus drive north of Cotton Plant, Arkansas. I recall her saying, "I clawed my way out of Cotton Plant." Her academic ability—she was high school valedictorian—got her out of what I'm sure was grinding poverty. Gloria grew up in a hard neighborhood and would not return to it. Jim was raised in a beautiful home in a prestigious old money neighborhood in Tulsa, Oklahoma, yet he chose to live in the middle of rural poverty, the environment Gloria had fled. She had no children of her own but helped raise a couple of nieces and nephews who she referred to as knuckleheads. She had worked for a long time at the department of social security, holding supervisory positions. She said she was blessed. She said she had had a good life but I wondered what she left out of her story.

Ella was the daughter of a Central High School basketball coach I was familiar with even though he had been retired for years. Her aunt was Joycelyn Elders, Surgeon General. Gloria had to coax her to reveal that she had been a celebrated athlete, a sharpshooting basketball player. She didn't last long in college. I am never surprised when former college athletes tell me they had to quit because of knee injuries, because mine got operated on my junior year at Ouachita. Ella admitted that she often wondered if she should have become a coach. She wore a nice gold bracelet on her wrist, but like the rest of us, there was no jewelry on her hands. I wondered what she was leaving out.

Jim told his story, leaving out some things, not that there was scandal. He had never done time or was ever the subject of restraining orders or was bankrupt, but he did say he had no children and was divorced, an understatement I had to overlook. That third divorce is hard to admit to. He also did not mention the qualities that made him an extraordinary person. Not every man can tell a modest rendition of his life story to nice looking women. That urge to impress them gets tedious, once you start identifying it. You realize you're still that little boy on the monkey bars at recess, trying to impress a cute girl who couldn't care less. It's an embarrassing insight.

After dinner I got to worrying about that freezing rain. A good amount of it on a vehicle will make it impregnable. We decided to pull the tarps off two firewood piles and throw them on our vehicles. Jim and I argued. "It's a one man job," I insisted, a little forceful maybe because by that time I was mildly drunk, but he had been trying to hide his limping all day. Gloria got all emotional, like I was trying to sneak across the border into North Korea and would never be seen again. Then Ella said, "I'll go with him. There's some things I want out of a bag." Jim and Gloria said that was a good idea. I protested, but it was feeble.

Gloria dressed Ella like she was her lady in waiting. Old kayakers collect cold weather clothing. Ella went out the door wearing everything but Mac's wet suit. All that nylon made a whispering sound as she walked beside me down the lane. It was that quiet. We kept the flashlight beams on the trail in front of us, careful to stay in the tracks we had made that morning. The cold pressed on my thighs and torso, but my face and fingertips felt a pinch. It was ten degrees, the sky open, a late phase moon hanging in the eastern sky. I asked Ella if she was okay. She said she was fine. We stopped at the top of the mountain where Jim's lane came out of the timber and joined the forest Service road. By the time we got there my head felt clear.

"Look. No lights."

"I can't believe the stars," she said. "I've never seen anything like this."

"The word awesome is overused, but I think you can say that the Milky Way tonight is an awesome sight."

"I guess this is why your friend lives up here, for sights like this."

"Nah. He moves farther back in the boonies every time he gets a divorce."

"Why does he do that?"

"'Proverbs 21, 19. It is better to live in the Wilderness than with an angry and contentious woman."

Her laugh had the usual tonic effect.

"He's such a nice guy. Were they all angry and contentious? And how many were there?"

I was surprised by her curiosity. Was she intrigued by him?

"All I'll say is that they were good gals," I replied. "Like mine. I can tell you all about my exes, but then you'd have to follow suit. Do we want to spill our guts, as the saying goes?"

"Nope. That won't be necessary."

"Good decision," I said.

"Gloria really likes Jim. For a friend I mean. Right away, too." She shook her head. "She hasn't said anything to me but it's very obvious because she usually keeps men at arm's length. It is very surprising."

"Smart girl. Lots of guys who don't like women are attracted to them. Physically anyway. Bad combination. I take it that Gloria is single."

She hesitated. "She has a friend. I'm not sure about how they feel about each other. I'm freezing," she said. "Let's go."

We said nothing else for a while. We took big downhill strides through the deep snow on the road. By the time we got to the Cherokee we were relieved to get in and warm it up. It took a while. The air got hot but every surface in the car was frozen. Our faces stung. Ella dug around in the back seat and retrieved a cloth shoulder bag. I cleared the snow off the windshield, made sure the wipers were free, and cleared the roof before I draped the tarp over the top, making sure the driver's side door was covered. I weighted the tarp down with a tackle box I found behind the back seat. It was inadequate but it was something. It was nice to be busy. Sitting practically shoulder to shoulder next to Ella in the front seat while the car warmed up was awkward. It was too quiet.

I got plenty winded going back up, though the trek seemed shorter, as hikes do when you've covered the ground a few times. It was too cold for sweat to pour down my back and wet my hair, so when we stopped to rest at the top of the hill I didn't start to shiver. Damp clothes will kill you at ten degrees, but I was dry and warm from the walk. We faced the south again as we caught our breath, admiring the mountains which went away to the horizon, dimly visible in the moonlight. The Milky Way glittered. "Hey," Ella said, as she turned to face me. She stepped forward and placed her elbows on my shoulders, pressing the back of my neck, which I bent to her willingly as her mouth met mine. She kissed me lightly, a caress more than a kiss, then she opened her mouth, just a little at first. Her mouth tasted minty. I was startled and slow to respond, but I wanted to encourage her so I dropped her bag and placed my hands about where her hips would be under all those clothes.

It turned out to be one of the best kisses of my life. I submitted to her. It was the first time a woman kissed me unexpectedly, but that can't account for the reaction I felt, which happened only after we stepped back from each other. The effect of her kisses was extraordinary, which is a mystery I've thought about many times, because while she kissed me skillfully, her technique and her anatomy, to put it mechanically, were not unusual. She did nothing other girls and women haven't done. She was different, even exotic, but people are people. I can't explain my reaction. To be sure I enjoyed it lots while it was happening. It was exciting and flattering but there was not in it a promise of delights to come and I do not recollect that it was sensual. Plus, it was brief, lasting maybe twenty seconds, before she bit my lower lip gently before unclasping her arms and stepping back.

I stammered, trying to make a joke. "Is the snow melting around my feet?"

"Let's go," she said. "I'm freezing."

As we walked back down the lane to the cabin something like a charism washed over me. I felt fortified with understanding and clarity. I felt reassured that virtue and goodness would start to prevail in my life. I realized then that I had been feeling trapped inside myself for a long time. Women have a marvelous ability to make men feel good. They've done this for me off and on all my life, but what happened to me on that mountaintop was like a laying on of hands. I was energized to be a better person. Maybe Ella's touch was a relief response from God who disguises his gifts. He knew I was struggling. I never got close to understanding it.

I knew intuitively that Ella and I would be content to mostly ignore each other for the rest of the time we would be together and we did just that. I'm pretty sure she didn't feel what I felt. For me, another kiss would be carnal, canceling the spiritual transmission of the embrace in the snow. Later, I decided that she wasn't supposed to feel what I felt. She was a messenger or courier. She might have thought that was absurd, but Gloria would have understood. Of course, the elation part didn't last. A day later I was grounded, though still fortified. Ordinary life intrudes, which is probably good. I turned a corner, but I'm back to living with spells of melancholy and frustration. They are part of life, and I could hardly drive to Little Rock, knock on Ella's door and say, "Um, remember me? Can I get a booster shot?"

The next day followed like the first. It was still too cold to get out much. I did walk the dogs, out to the road and back once in the morning and once in the evening. Just before dark the mutts and I walked down to the bluff which overlooks the pasture but the elk were gone. After lunch Jim explained to me why Eugene Onegin is so great, so I gave it another try, reading it for an hour before concluding that what would really give me pleasure would be to feed Pushkin to the wood stove. I still felt buoyant and positive but as the day proceeded I lost interest in my surroundings, to say the least, so I accessed my school's software website on Jim's laptop, looked at my grade book and lesson plans, something I never do at home. I change the date on my lesson plans and turn in the same ones every year. They looked pretty bad so I cleaned them up till that got tedious. You'd have thought Jim and Gloria went to high school together, the way they continued to get along. I thought it was a bit much when she talked to him through the bathroom door, but maybe I was envious.

The next day, at mid-morning, we heard yelling out front. We stopped what we were doing and lifted our heads, like deer which hear a twig snap. I got to the door first. A big, yellow road grader as long as the cabin filled the lot, a marvel to look at. Its plexiglass door flew open, revealing a bearded man in coveralls. "Jim, get your car off the road!" he roared. "I bladed around it!"

Jim sidled around me down the steps as fast as he could. "Danny Brown! Can I get up the mountain to my lane?"

"Oh, yeah."

"You're early," Jim said.

"Dry snow and fourteen hour days."

"What's seven look like?"

"If you're headed south you're good. You cain't get down the mountain to Jasper till tomorrow. Maybe not then. That freezing rain is still in the forecast."

"My company is headed south. That's good. I appreciate you," Jim said. "You want coffee?"

"Nah, I don't need no more. I'm stopping to pee like an old bird dog already. We'll see you.

"That man means more to me than my congressman or the governor," Jim said, admiration in his voice, as the grader left the lot. "The girls will be delighted. I'd like to see them way south of here by dark. I'll go in and call that wrecker and see if he can't help us out."

"That forecast makes me nervous," I said. "Let's get going."

So I fetched the car while the girls packed. Jim's hero could have told me I needed a shovel. I had to kick snow out of the way to open the car door and for a while the car wouldn't budge but I rocked it back and forth and backed up till it was free. The road was not entirely free of snow but I made it to the top. Jim and the women loaded up into a warm car. I followed them to the highway, a load of snow in the back of my truck and on the roof and hood. Highway 7 was bladed and passable. What snow was on it was dirty and ground up. When the sun went down the pavement would re-freeze. If the wrecker winched Gloria's car up the hillside without trouble, the gals and I would be on dry pavement in an hour. When we got near Cowell I wouldn't have known where Gloria's car was but for the wrecker which sat waiting by the side of the road. The driver stood behind the wrecker, looking down the hill at the Impala. Jim and I pulled in behind him. I moved some stuff from the front seat to the back, took a gulp of coffee, and got out just in time to see the driver get back in his truck. Jim was standing by the open door of his Cherokee, his hands in the air, watching as the wrecker drove away.

"What is happening?" I said as I approached him.

He closed the door and turned to meet me. He looked grim. In a low voice he said, "He walked up to the car, said, 'Howdy, sir,' then he looked in the car at our friends, turned around and left."

I felt sick, helpless and angry at the same time. "Jesus. What can we do?"

"His shop is in Deer. I'm pretty sure I know where it is. Let's go talk to him. We'll leave the girls here in my car."

When he got in my truck I said, "What did you tell them?"

"I said I didn't know what was going on. I told them I was going to see a man about a dog and I'd be back in under an hour."

"They know what's up, don't they?"

"Sure. That son of a bitch."

It wasn't far to Deer, but I didn't need much time to think about what was going to happen. Gloria's car would be pulled up to the highway or Jim McReynolds would get his pound of flesh. By the time we pulled into the parking lot of Wilson Automotive I had had plenty of time to ponder the fact I that I was following an old pal who had the personality of a Scottish clan chieftain from the seventeenth century, bent on conflict with a knuckle- dragging redneck, that I'd be involved in it, and on my own, I don't experience much conflict. There were a half a dozen vehicles in the front lot and a wrecker in the back. We opened the door and strolled in. It looked like the owners of the vehicles were all inside. Of course the conversation stopped. This wasn't a franchise operation with a nice waiting room with a coffee maker and Ducks Unlimited magazines on a coffee table. The place was a mess: ramshackle chairs, automotive parts manuals in stacks. Cardboard boxes labeled "antifreeze" were piled up next to one end of the desk. A doorway led to the shop area. I scanned the room. The crowd in there would have made a good pirate crew if you switched out their seafarer costumes for square-toed boots, Carhartt jackets, jeans and feed caps. Guys from Deer, Arkansas, grow beards like Russians. Behind a desk by the back wall, a man about my age sat facing us. His mopey face and long sideburns gave him an Airedale look. He was the only man of that crew who did not have a beard. Radiating confidence, he looked us up and down as Jim approached the desk. I hated him. It seemed prudent, I don't know why, to stand back a pace or two from Jim. Three or four guys were out of sight behind me, but I could see two men out of the corner of my eyes, one to my right and one to my left. The guy on my left was gaunt, grey, and exhausted looking, dwarfed by a big coat. He wore a Vietnam Veteran hat. A younger guy on the right concerned me. I can describe him in two words-- interior lineman.

"Would you be Mr. Wilson?"

"I am."

"Sir," Jim began, "I called you three days ago and arranged to have your wrecker meet me in Cowie when the roads cleared. I spoke to you again a couple of hours ago. I thought we had an understanding. I'm afraid you left when we arrived. May I have an explanation?" Jim's demeanor was formal, his voice soft and polite.

Wilson leaned back in his chair. He looked relaxed. He had an audience. He was going to have some fun. He did not know Jim but he was probably convinced that Jim looked down on him, simply because Jim was "not from around here." Jim had large, almond shaped eyes and a dome forehead, the face of an intellectual, a mug you see on a roman bust. There were seventeen inches of snow on the ground and he was in socks and Teva sandals, khakis and a baggy sweater and he was polite. I'm pretty sure Wilson thought he was looking at a weak man.

"No, you may not," Wilson said, in a mocking tone. He stressed the word "may" and used his fingers to put quotation marks around it. His voice was hoarse.

Jim shuffled toward the desk till his thighs rested against it. He leaned over and placed his hands on the desk top. Jim looked down; Wilson looked up. "Chomp my balls, butt breath pig f——ker," Jim said, companionably, to Wilson's upturned face.

"HeeeeeeHeeeeee….." from the interior lineman. Jim started around the corner of the desk. Wilson rose, rage in his face. There was a lot of yelling. The Vietnam vet came at me. I could not ignore him but I wanted to watch Jim. In my opinion, boxing is a bad sport which needs to go away but Jim was a fine amateur fighter and I love to watch a good athlete do anything. What Jim could do which is rare was slip jabs and straight rights, bob under hooks and counterpunch with stinging accuracy. He could not hit hard and did not have a great cardiovascular system but he frustrated opponents with his ability to stay close to them without getting tagged, meanwhile throwing combinations to the head and body. The Vietnam vet closed on me, lowered his head even with my chest and began to throw slow, crab like punches at where he thought I was standing. His coat rode up on his head and shoulders. I shoved him aside, the poor old guy. "HeeeeeeeHeeeee" from the interior lineman. I looked at Wilson in time to see the surprise on his face as Jim reached the back of the desk. Wilson realized that Jim was not going to chest-bump and bluster until someone separated them. Wilson was penned behind his desk and the wall. He tumbled over his chair trying to get away. I couldn't see him on the floor behind the desk but I had a pretty good idea that he wouldn't be getting up till Jim left.

"Look out, Mac!" I yelled. Jim turned to face two guys from behind me who rushed him. Honestly, looking back, I think they were trying to break up the nonsense, but they were on Jim with their hands in the air. Jim knocked them off their feet. They hopped up quickly, looking shocked and sheepish. One of them actually grinned.

"HeeeeeeheeeeeHehHehHehHeeeee " from the interior lineman.

I yelled, "Stop! Stop! We'll go!"

From the floor behind the desk I heard Wilson say, "I've got bronchitis," in a pity-poor-me voice.

Jim whirled around, looked down, delivered an order. "Shut up, piss ant." No fool, he gave lots of room to the two guys he knocked to the floor as he walked past them. "Good day, gents," he said. I believe we got out of there without further incident, even though he had just knocked those fellows to the floor, because he sounded like he meant it.

I was elated when we got to the parking lot, happy that my jaw wasn't broken. Thanks to my friend, I had a memory which would warm my heart for Christmases to come, even if it was a comedy instead of a Nativity drama. Jim was muttering complaints and chuckling at the same time. We looked at each other before we reached my truck. What to do about Gloria's car? What would we tell the women? The conversation would be humiliating and the trip back to Jim's cabin with them would be grim. We glanced back at the door to Wilson Automotive, then shook our heads. There was no reason to linger in Deer, Arkansas. We were getting in my truck when we heard "Hey boys!"

The lineman approached us. "Let's go get that car," he said.

"Can you help us?" Jim said. "How?"

He pointed to a mud-splattered Dodge Ram with dual wheels, facing us. It menaced my little Toyota four cylinder. Its big mirrors stuck out of the cab like horns on a bison. A winch the size of a footlocker was bolted to the front bumper. "Brand new Talon winch. You hook it up," he said. "I can't get under a car."

Jim exhaled. "Mister, I can't tell you how much I appreciate this," he said, relief pouring out of him. "We'll pay you for your trouble."

"No, you won't. Sorry about Jay. I know you don't believe me but the truth is he's a pretty good old boy. He's just ignorant. He's my father-in-law. His daughter's gonna chew his ass out when she hears about this."

We followed the Dodge Ram to Cowell. Jim unspooled the cable from the winch down the hill to the Impala while the lineman and I stood at the edge of the pavement and watched. The days are gone when you can wrap a chain or a cable around a bumper. Jim had to burrow under the car and connect to openings in the frame behind the bumper. There was no room to maneuver. His upper body was out of sight but his legs thrashed as he pushed packed snow out behind him. It took a while and it had to have been a miserable job. When he emerged he had snow in his sweater, in his hair, on his khakis and I know down his collar. He was panting and shaking his frozen hands. By that time Gloria had joined us. She started to squawk. The lineman just laughed. "You don't have to worry about that one."

I just shook my head. "He wouldn't have it any other way," I said.

Jim opened the car and started it. The Talon winch labored till the Impala broke free of the drifts around it. In two minutes the car was on pavement. Victory! In ten minutes the gals were gone.

It is unusual for me to pass by Haw Creek Falls without stopping but there were patches of snow on the ground and I had had enough of that so I zipped past the place on the trip home. I did have the happy thought as I drove by that if our new friends came up in early summer we'd show them the falls. We'd sit in lawn chairs in the shallow water above the falls and have a glass of wine. We'd sit with our feet in the water and laugh about being cooped up in Jim's place during the blizzard. It was a nice daydream. Okay, I couldn't help it: yeah, I thought about how much fun it would be to pull Ella close to me by the falls under the stars on a soft summer night, Ella now in shorts, sandals and a sleeveless top, but time is more relentless than even desire. We never saw those nice women again.

"Crystal's History"
Mark Burnett

II

Break-In On Clifton Court

I was awake at 3:00 a.m., one fretful idea after another crowding my mind, when I heard a crashing sound coming from my garage. At the same time I thought I heard a car or truck motor in the alley and I realized that I might have been hearing that sound, a low rumble, for a while. Momentarily, the distraction was a relief. It got me away from the monkeys jumping around in my head, each one waving an idea on a banner, the main one if I should get out of coaching and become an administrator for the rest of my career. I've never been good at shaking unwanted ideas.

I listened for the crashing sound again. That noise didn't repeat, but when I concentrated on the motor sound I was sure I could still hear it. Naturally, the flashlight wasn't where it was supposed to be. Living alone, who could I blame for that? The aluminum baseball bat that stays close by in the hall closet felt snug in my hand as I went down my porch steps and crossed the concrete parking between my house and my detached garage, going out to do battle wearing boxers and flip-flops. My friends tell me I need a gun. The neighborhood has deteriorated, can't deny it, but I've overreacted every time I broke up a fight at school, slinging kids around and yelling. I probably shouldn't own a gun. A bat is a beast of a weapon, and besides, I'd never had a break-in.

I trotted across the lawn to the privet hedge which runs along my back fence, ducking under the garage window, to the back gate where I could see a big pickup truck with a ladder rack idling in the alley, lights off. The back gate stays dummy locked. I slipped the lock out of the latch and let myself through. On the other side of the trash cans the back door to my garage was open a crack, and I could hear stuff being moved around. In the dim light I could see that the door jamb was pried open. Feeling good about having the element of surprise and figuring I could end this little party by evicting one guest at a time, I leaned the bat against the gate and frog-walked low around the back of the truck until I reached the driver's door. Standing up, I gripped the ladder rack with my right hand, and punched him with my left hand through the open window. I'm a righty, but I got him pretty good though his face turned away some when I let him have it. I planted my feet to get him again when the truck lurched forward, stopped and took off. Holding the ladder rack, I ran alongside the truck punching him over and over in the face and side of the head, missing mostly but hitting some. He stopped hard and I slammed into the door. My left arm and part of my chest went inside the window for a second. It hurt. He put his arm and elbow up by the side of his face and tried to lean away as I kept hitting him. Then he stuck something out the window, pointed up. A gun went off by the side of my head. I pushed away and fell, stumbling back against a chain link fence, a yapping dog barking its head off behind me. I lay there in something like shock for a minute. When I got up the tail lights of the truck were turning right onto Kinkead. Someone ran down the alley in the other direction. The neighborhood sounded like a kennel. The incident shook me up. My last fight had been on an elementary school playground. Needless to say, that one didn't end with a gun going off by my ear. I had used bad judgment but I got away with it and felt a sense of victory.

I hit the light switch just inside the door. Crystal's stuff was scattered everywhere. The drawers to her dresser were turned upside down. The big entertainment center doors were wide open. A laundry basket filled with assorted items--bills, a cheap jewelry box, an iron--stuff I dumped in there when I hauled her things to my garage after she moved out of my rent house, was empty, the contents dumped on my workbench. A crowbar, not mine, lay on the floor just inside the door. None of my stuff was touched. My golf clubs, tools, and my good fly rods were where they were supposed to be. I hammered the jamb back into place good enough to shut and lock the door, went inside, and went to bed.

I had only been in bed a little over an hour when I had heard the crashing sounds in my garage, having been too revved up to sleep, though I was pretty tired. Coach Bagwell had us watching films till one-thirty after Pine Bluff had beat us like a drum the evening before. By the time I got home, made the coffee and dropped my clothes on the bedroom floor, I only had time to sleep about an hour before I woke up, mulling over whether I wanted to stay in coaching. Now I had less than two hours till the paperboy pitched the Arkansas Democrat Gazette onto my sidewalk, a long time to brood over what those sorry sons of bitches were doing in my garage, going through Crystal Lambeth's stuff. The only thing I had found in her stuff that was interesting, and I admit I went through everything but her panty drawer, was her partially filled out application to be a Dallas Cowboy Cheerleader, and it was interesting only because it was pathetic. That thought got interrupted by the realization that they probably were after her drugs. Obvious as it was, it took me a while to figure it out and when I did it didn't help me get to sleep.

Officer Weintraub was on the phone when I walked into her tiny office on Monday morning after cross-country practice. Wedged between the principal's office and the counseling center, her office must have seen its first use as a janitor's closet. She pointed to the chair. I sat down, squeezed between the wall and her desk. She was nodding her head while she tapped a pencil eraser on her desk calendar, the phone at her ear.

"So you don't remember her, don't remember talking to her," Weintraub was saying. There was doubt in her voice. "She says she knows you. You sure? Yep, a sophomore here at Northside. And like I said, I'm Northside's resource officer, Fort Smith P.D. Mmhmm. I'm sure you do talk to lots of girls. Well, I've got her phone in front of me. Looks like you've been texting her. Now you remember! Good. Jason, how old are you? Eighteen? That's a problem. What? I said, 'that's a problem.' Hold on, Jason, someone just walked in. Don't hang up. I've got to tell this person something. Don't hang up."

She pressed her phone to her chest. Whatever was there, compressed behind a bullet proof vest, was a source of speculation among the coaches.

"I'm going to let him sweat for a minute. Give him a chance to decide to tell me the truth. I got your email. You're lucky you weren't shot. You should have called the cops."

"Right."

"You've got a situation."

"I know it."

"They're looking for drugs," she said.

"It could have been worse. I got a fridge full of beer out there."

"You better take this seriously."

I was taking it seriously. I'm highly skilled at pretending to listen to women, this from eating lunch in a teacher's lounge for ten years, but she had my attention. She knows what's up.

She went back to the phone conversation, her voice friendly. I watched her, a pretty brunette. She had nice eyebrows, a detail you don't often notice. Like every policewoman I have ever seen, she looked uncomfortable in her uniform. I wondered, was it physical, being cinched up so tight, or could it be psychological? Sometimes women coaches act hard-ass when they coach just to show the world they can make it in a male world. Do women cops stand sideways in front of a mirror, holding their tummies in while they adjust their mace and weapon? Regardless, she's all cop, I thought.

"Sorry, Jason. Like I said, there is a problem. I'm glad you remember Candace. You told her you have some killer smoke. That would be marijuana. That would be contributing to the delinquency of a minor." She paused for a few seconds. "Don't forget I'm scrolling through her texts."

There was nothing on her desk but some files. "You think you might have. Maybe? Just joking around? I see. You didn't mean it. Yes. Yes. Jason, let me tell you…Jason, I.…Jason! Don't interrupt. Listen to me!"

She's on the firing range, I thought, shooting rounds through a target. Weintraub lowered her voice and spoke slowly. "She's fifteen years old. You're eighteen, if you aren't lying. Do you want to end up in court? Remember, you're eighteen, this is big boy court. What? Good. You're going to delete her number and forget you ever met Candace Thompson, aren't you? Good. If you ever need anything you call me but you forget about Candace, okay? You're welcome, Jason. Goodbye." Weintraub dropped her phone on her desk, looked at me, and shook her head.

"Did you get his attention?" I asked.

"Maybe. He didn't try to tell me he didn't know she was under-age. That's a good sign. If he wasn't scared he's a good actor. What do you need, Ed?"

"I'm on Clifton Court, 800 block, halfway between Grand and Kinkead. You know that, right? Well, there's a beer joint at 34th and Grand, The Farewell Party. I check out the parking lot every time I drive by cause I got a friend who practically lives there. I got a habit of looking for his truck. Yesterday there was an older pickup with a ladder rack parked in front of the joint. Can you run the tag?"

"There's a hundred of those in Fort Smith."

"That's right."

She leaned back in her chair. "I'm not supposed to do that."

"Never mind. I shouldn't have asked," I said. I shrugged. "Say, I've never seen you wear anything but a cop uniform. I've always thought you'd look great in a cocktail dress, something black and loose fitting. While you were on the phone I was thinking. I've never seen you in pearls. I bet you'd turn heads."

"Well, you'll never find out, Coach Wakefield." She came down hard on the word coach. "I swear, coaches are worse than cops. I'll run the tag and if there's something you really need to know I'll find a way of telling you."

She lifted her laptop off a shelf, placed it on the desk and un-folded it. "By the way," she said. "I do remember Crystal. She was a cheerleader. Just her sophomore year, I think. She wasn't typical, which is why I remember her. Beverly Wilson was the cheer spon-sor. She used to talk about her all the time. Crystal car dated in ju-nior high and had a two a.m. curfew."

I shook my head.

"Why did you rent to her?"

"My Vietnamese neighbor across the street sold me the house. He's a friend. She came with it."

Weintraub looked up from the laptop. She frowned in concentration. Those cute eyebrows went up and down as she stared hard into space. "Her grandmother...hmm, yeah, it was her. Her grandmother worked in our cafeteria for a while."

"Do you remember her name?"

"Nooo," she said slowly. "But I'll call Beverly. She'll know." She looked at her laptop. "Bobby Hopkins. Pocola, Oklahoma. No arrest record. Forget him." She sighed. "You should have called the police. I can't believe no one in your neighborhood did."

"After the dogs quit barking I guess everyone went back to sleep. I could have lain in the alley all night in my underwear, a bullet in my head."

"You need to get that stuff out of your garage. I assume you went through it."

"Couldn't find a thing. I don't think there was ever anything there, but maybe that clown that ran down the alley had it in his hand. I screwed up when I went after the driver. I should have gone in the garage with my bat and tenderized that dirt bag 's head. If I yard sale her stuff or take it to Goodwill, then what? What do I do, put a note on the door? I got to find Crystal and tell her she needs to come get her stuff and tell her friends."

"What you should have done is call the cops. Ed, whoever is after her dope isn't going to hear it from her that you don't have it. She's better off with them thinking you have it. And think about why she hasn't been back. She's laying low."

I didn't want to hear that I was being used for Crystal's convenience, especially as I was doing her a favor. I wasn't going to mention it to Heather, but one reason I kept Crystal's stuff was I felt sorry for her. She didn't impress me as being very smart or having much common sense. I figured she'd come get the rest of her things a few days after I evicted her. I'd taken her to small claims court and had her car impounded till she came up with the back rent she owed. Selling her stuff, even though she left it in my house, didn't seem necessary. I had space in the garage and moved everything from across the street in two hours with my neighbor Corey helping me because I wanted to paint the rental and have Carmelita clean. After which, it looked like Crystal set me up.

"It's too late to call the cops now, isn't it?"

"Probably. I called Detective Eversole. He wanted to know about it. They're not going to do anything but you need to know what he told me."

"I know, I know. I almost got shot and I should have called the cops."

"Listen. After all those shootings and home invasions in Springdale, law enforcement is bird dogging the Hispanic gangs up there. Well guess what, the trend to move from Fort Smith to Northwest Arkansas for employment opportunities is being reversed. We're enrolling Hispanic boys who are bad news. Their parents don't look like our Hispanic parents. These people make our meth crowd look reasonable, and of course our guys are jumpy."

"They're going to start shooting each other, aren't they?" I said.

"Some stuff's already been happening which hasn't made the papers. I'm not one of these people who thinks everyone needs to be carrying, but Ed, you probably need some protection at home."

"The best thing would be for you to stay with me for a few days and protect me."

"And I guess you'd take me to The Farewell Party at 34th and Grand. Is that where I'm supposed to wear that cocktail dress?" Smiling, she laced her fingers together and rested her chin on her hands. "My bottom line for being a bodyguard is usually a seven day cruise to Cancun, but I'll think about giving you a break. Because I like you so much."

I had a good rest of the week. We got a great rain at night early in the week which broke the hot spell. I've got some cross-country kids who would show up and run even if I missed practice, and keeping those kids academically eligible is a snap. The kids ran hard. I got five or six real athletes, enough to compete in the meets, but I also have a bunch of overweight kids who really try. You have to like them. It doesn't matter to me if they are slow. Basketball coaches really don't want a bunch of kids who can't help out because they get in the way, but cross-country coaches don't have to cut kids. Another thing I like is I never saw their parents. You can't argue with stopwatch times. Frustrated football parents, on the other hand, let you know you should be playing their son more, and can't understand why our whole staff is blind to all that blazing talent. After Coach Nichols came back from surgery on Wednesday, Coach Bagwell told me he just needed me on game days. I'm getting to where I hate football practice, though the games are still fun, and anyway the week went fast.

On Friday, Heather texted me. "I talked to Bev. Crystal's gran is Audra Shepherd. 501 Alabama? Leave Bev's name out." The 500 block of Alabama is spitting distance from my house. I went by there right after school on Friday. It was a nice early fall afternoon. The evenings were cooling off. Everyone was afraid we'd have a poor foliage display because it had been so dry so long but I was starting to notice a red maple or two in my neighborhood in the early stages of turning crimson.

501 Alabama sat on a fifty foot lot like mine but was smaller than my house, and covered with old metal siding which needed power washing. Some Nandina bushes out front and a couple of those retro outdoor chairs made of sheet metal and bent pipe on the porch told me an old person lived there. The space under the carport was empty but I knocked on her front door anyway, triggering a tiny dog yapping inside. I wondered how many were in there. A tall woman in a pink house coat opened the door and peered at me through the storm door glass. Her plump, sagging face looked like

it had been moistened and dusted with powder from the same end of the color spectrum as her pink housecoat and orange hair. Her rouge spots were like shields. Her dogs scratched the bottom of the storm door as they yapped away. I don't know of a more annoying sound.

"Mrs. Shepherd, I used to be Crystal's landlord. She's got a bunch of stuff in my garage. Can you tell her I'll let her have it if she'll come get it? I'd appreciate it." Of course when I started talking, those damned dogs got even louder. I had to yell over them. You could have heard me on the basketball courts at Tilles Park.

She ignored the noise. I hate animal cruelty as much as the next guy, but I was having bad thoughts about those dogs.

She leaned forward. "Who are you? Who told you where I live?"

"Ed Wakefield," I yelled. "Crystal's landlord. She needs to come by my house."

"Who told you where I live?"

I lie with confidence when it's justified. "One of the cooks in our cafeteria at Northside remembers you. She thought you still lived here. I know Crystal would like to have her stuff back."

"I don't see my granddaughter. Who told you how to find me?"

She knew I was lying. I was caught. I was surprised and a little embarrassed. I said, "Never mind, ma'am. I'm sorry I bothered you," as polite as I could even though I was irritated. As I turned away, I heard the door close. It felt good to get away from that damned yapping.

As I backed out of the carport and turned up Alabama, I saw her next door neighbor parked in his yard--a tall young man in a beard who was pulling a kayak out of the back of his truck. He had that lean, rangy build you see in triathletes that makes me think of a leaf spring. We made eye contact and nodded. He had on river shoes, nylon pants with cargo pockets and a tee shirt with that big tongue from the Rolling Stone album cover on the front. I pulled up to the curb and turned the motor off.

"Been on the Mulberry?"

"Nope. Paddled the Frog," he said. "Lancaster to Rudy. Had a good day. Don't get to float in September too often. " He sounded satisfied.

"I floated sixty miles of the Buffalo last Spring Break. Middle of the week, didn't see hardly anybody."

"Sweet."

"I guess you heard that conversation."

He laughed. "Well, yeah, I heard it."

"How do you stand those dogs?"

"Don't get me started. I talked to her about it. Tried to anyway. I'm moving soon."

"Do you know Crystal? Her granddaughter?"

"She the one in the white Mustang with the pink stripes on the hood? "

"Yeah. She used to rent from me. You heard all that. Trouble."

He shook his head. "I see her over there once or twice a week. I tried to talk to her once, but she wouldn't even make eye contact with me. She's not bad looking, but to tell the truth, she probably ain't my type."

"You're probably right. I don't think you could get her to float the Mulberry with you on a pretty day. She's probably more of a hot tub at 2 a.m. type of gal."

"Well, that might not be too bad," he said with a grin. He probably wasn't kidding. Whitewater paddlers are not cautious types.

"Just don't rent to her. If you see her, would you mind telling her that I wish she'd come get her stuff out of my garage? I don't know if that old lady will give her the message though I don't know why she wouldn't."

"Come to think of it, I haven't seen her in a week or two. But I'll tell her if I see her. Have a good one, man."

I went home and got on the couch, intending to get off my feet and try to relax for an hour before I headed to the field house. I always get keyed up on game day. When I was a kid I didn't sleep well the nights before a game. We hadn't won much the last couple of years, but before that, for decades, Northside fielded great football teams. I hated these losing seasons. Coaches can't use the excuse year after year that they don't have any talent, though in our case it was true. A look at a Northside yearbook would show you that we are a soccer school now, not a football school. Our good black athletes were starting to transfer to Southside, leaving us our Mexican kids.

Laying in bed, staring at the ceiling fan, I thought about the day Kiet walked up to my porch and told me he wanted me to buy his rent house, which was across the street from mine. "You buy my how. I give you good pri. It a good how," he said. His raspy voice purred when he told me it was a good house. I knew he believed it. He was a true believer when it came to the properties he bought and sold. They were all jewels.

He held a Marlboro between fingers not much bigger than the cigarette itself. An immigrant on his way to be a millionaire if cancer didn't kill him, he had on torn, paint-splattered clothes, predictable as the cigarette he was smoking down to the filter. He had a son in medical school and a pharmacist daughter who would inherit dozens of rental properties on the north side of Fort Smith. We were pretty friendly and I had reason to trust him. He thought the rental business was a gold mine and he encouraged me, sometimes to the point of being annoying, to get in on the bonanza. He did give me a good price.

I told him I thought his tenant used to be a student at my school. I swear he said she paid the rent on time and never asked for anything. It didn't matter now, but it still bugged me that he told me that. Looking back, nothing about renting to Crystal added up. I spent a lot of time thinking about her, maybe because I felt like I brought this on myself, and because of what happened to her, but I got nowhere figuring it out.

I left the house early to go by Coleman Pharmacy. When I went in I saw Crystal at the counter talking to Mike the pharmacist. As I stood there looking at her, I had the sour thought that she was in there to get prescription painkillers, courtesy of some quack doctor in Oklahoma, where I knew from looking at her stuff that she was in bondage to payday loan companies. I went outside and leaned against the building, finally noticing her car in the back. In a few minutes she came out, in a hurry, but empty handed. I got loud before she saw me. "Crystal! Come here!" She looked scared but she walked toward me. Thinner than I last saw her, she had on white pants, gold sandals and a red sleeveless tee shirt. Her pony tail was stuck through a ball cap, the brim pulled down over her forehead. The brim bobbed up and down as she talked. She wouldn't make eye contact with me. She looked tired.

"I'm going to pay you," she said. "I'm sorry. I'm really, really sorry. I got a job at Red Lobster and they didn't pay me for all my hours and..."

"Crystal. Hush. You don't owe me any money." Who wants to listen to lies?

"I don't? But..."

"I kept your deposit and got a check from the sheriff's department when you got your car out of impoundment. You don't owe me any money. I want you to come get your stuff." I got loud again for the next part, not football practice loud, but loud enough that she flinched. "Now. Right now, Crystal. Follow me to my house and start putting your crap in your car. Dump it on your granny's porch.

If you don't come get the big stuff tomorrow I'm putting it on the curb."

"You'll let me have it?"

"Let you have it? Crystal,....come....get.....your.......stuff! Jesus!" I had more to say but it looked like she was starting to get weepy.

"Oh, thank you. Thank you, coach."

She followed me to my driveway. I parked in front of the house, waved her up the drive to the garage, following her on foot. I lifted up the overhead garage door and motioned her in.

"Start loading the small stuff. I had a break-in the other night. I moved my tools and fly rods inside, but they weren't after my stuff. They reason your stuff is scattered everywhere is whoever broke in went through it. We both know what that means. I've got to go. It's game night. Lower that overhead door when you leave. Push the lever down to lock it."

"Yes, sir. Thank you. I'm sorry...I"

I made my voice as cold as I could. "Crystal, you've got some enemies. Do you want another one?"

"Nooo." The brim bobbed as her eyes cut right and left. She looked wary and sounded scared.

"Then you tell all your friends you got your stuff out of my garage. All of them. You post it tonight on Facebook or Instagram, whatever. I'll find out if you haven't done it."

We upset Cabot that night, a big win. Our offense executed well, the best all season. I was happy for the kids, and for Coach Bagwell, but Cabot helped us out. They made lots of mistakes. Part of my job is to keep people off the sidelines, mainly Coach Bagwell when he's hot after a ref, but I noticed that Cabot's outside linebacker and defensive end on the far side of the field were biting hard so I told coach about it. He called a reverse which set us up for a score. Not bad for a track coach, I told myself. After the kids went home, Bagwell told us we could look at game films on Monday after practice, so I pulled into my driveway about an hour before midnight. The Mustang was still back by the garage, which meant I had to park in front. It was apparent that Crystal was going to piss me off till the last opportunity. The garage door was down and locked, so I went straight in the house and went to bed. I expected that she'd be back at midnight, and make a lot of racket. Nothing was easy with her, but at least I got her started.

The next morning after I read the game scores with my coffee, I got curious about how much stuff she had moved, if any. When I walked past the Mustang I noticed that it was unlocked and empty. I raised the overhead door and stepped inside. She was lying between her entertainment center and a coffee table. At first it confused me. She looked so small I thought she was a child, a neighbor kid who got in my garage somehow, but at the same time I knew it was her. She lay there on the concrete like she was thrown down. The side of her head was bloody and beat in. I felt my breathing slow as I stared at her. I was relieved that I could not see her face. She looked utterly defenseless and vulnerable. I went from being mad at her to feeling so sorry for her. She didn't deserve anything like this. I felt sick with regret. I finally saw with clarity that she was raised crazy and wasn't very smart and couldn't get over it. When would I learn this? What kind of coach was I, what kind of teacher, that I always thought people should just shake off their past? I wondered if it was somehow my fault, my bad judgment, that she got killed. Everyone told me I screwed up by not calling the cops. If I had, would she be alive?

Then I realized I was thinking about myself, not her, so I went back to the porch steps, sat down and leaned forward, my elbows on my knees, my fingers laced on the back of my neck. "May her soul rest in peace," I murmured. "May her soul and the souls of all the faithful departed through the mercy of God rest in peace." The image of the dried blood in her hair at her temple and dented crown wrecked my concentration. I tried to say more but I was too shook up so I went inside to call the police.

I didn't sleep well that night or Sunday night. It was hard to think about anything other than Crystal getting killed in my garage. I don't believe there's anyone who can tell me how to shake off an unwanted thought. It's bothered me since I was a kid. The memory of Crystal on the garage floor dogged me. Plus, I thought a lot about that grandmother. People who aren't wrapped too tight have an even harder time with tragedy than people who are strong. I couldn't imagine how much grief was in that old woman's mind. I figured she was alone in that little house on Alabama, Crystal's stuff a bigger problem for her than it ever was for me. Whoever had done that to Crystal had done a cruel thing to Mrs. Shepherd.

On Monday morning, after cross-country practice, I took a sick day, went home and slept hard for six hours. I was still in a funk but I woke up feeling rested. I moved my stuff back out to the garage and tried to clean up the stain on my floor. I went to the bank and to Yeagers to get furnace filters. My last errand was to Coleman Pharmacy again to get the items I hadn't gotten Friday night. When I drove past The Farewell Party I saw Kirk's truck. Knowing that he was good at reviving people, I decided to drink a beer with him. After I parked and got out, I was startled to see the pickup truck with the ladder rack parked at the back side of the building, lined up with other vehicles. It was like it was sitting there waiting for me. It sounds crazy, but I took it as a taunt. Having Kirk in there made me bold, so I went inside.

You enter The Farewell Party through a side door. Just past the bathrooms is the bar, on the left, so you walk past the backs of a long row of guys. Two or three always lean back and look over their shoulders to see who came in. I didn't know any of them. The light was bad, the fixtures plastic promotional products from Budweiser and Coors, but I could see my buddy Kirk at a big table in the back.

Just as I reached the corner of the bar, a guy who was standing between two other guys sitting on bar stools turned to the person on
his left, showing me his profile. He had on khaki pants and a brown
tee shirt. His ball cap was on the back of his head, backwards, his
brown hair in bangs sweeping across his forehead. He was bruised
from temple to jaw. I felt like a camera bulb flashed in my face, but
I kept walking. My buddy was at a table with some old men who
weren't letting bad health get in the way of having a good time.
They were loud and the juke box was on. I stood behind Kirk, put
my hands on the straps of his overalls and leaned down, my mouth
at his ear. "The guy at the corner of the bar, standing up," I whis-
pered. "Don't look. His face is bruised. Does he drive a pickup with
a ladder rack?"

Kirk stared straight ahead for a second. He twisted and looked
up at me, giving me a cold stare which said we needed to talk. He
nodded his head yes and turned back. "Don't get me one yet," I said
over my shoulder as I walked away. I couldn't bear to walk past the
guy at the bar so I weaved through the tables on my way out.

When I got outside, I called Heather and asked her to send a cop
car my way. She sounded doubtful till I told her why. I moved my
truck near the truck with the ladder rack. I sat behind the wheel,
watching the door to the bar in my side mirror. I was nervous and
impatient for the cops to arrive and I hoped he wouldn't come out.
I rubbed my sweaty palms on my thighs, rocking a little till I made
myself quit.

He did come out of the bar, headed right to his vehicle. I got out
of mine quick and I met him at his tailgate.

"The cops are on the way to talk to you about killing Crystal
Lambeth. You're not getting in that truck."

He turned to face me. I had lots of weight on him, maybe forty
pounds, but he had a gun in the truck.

He chuckled. "You're crazy. Who the hell are you?" His voice was low and casual.

I still wasn't sure about it. I said, "If you try to get in that truck I'm going to tear up the other side of your face like I did last week."

The understanding and fear I saw in his expression took a burden off me. He tried to take off. I lunged at him. He hadn't rounded the corner of his tailgate when I closed in on him. I know how to wrap up somebody who's trying to get around me. As we were about to collide he turned to face me. I shoved him against his tailgate. We were thigh to thigh and groin to groin like we were mating, but I shoved his upper body away from me hard, my left hand squeezing his throat just under his jaw, my right arm around his back, pinning his left arm. His spine was bent back over the tailgate. His upper body was nearly horizontal. It would have broken my back. I hid my face in his shoulder. All he could do with his free hand was claw and swat at my wrist under his chin and the top of my head. He made gasping sounds in his nose and mouth but his body still struggled against me, so I stayed rigid, wondering how long he could keep it up. The swatting and the squirming were starting to get feeble when a voice across the parking lot yelled "Step back! Fort Smith Police! Step back!" I was glad to do it.

The funeral was on a Wednesday, the middle of the day. I struggled with whether I should go. It wasn't a good time to take off work and everyone knows funerals for young people who die suddenly are awful. A lot of people who were having miserable lives would be there. I decided to not go, but there were tremors in the underground passages of my subconscious where that strange creature, my conscience, lives. I settled them down with a compromise, by going to the visitation at Lewis Funeral Chapel on Kelley Highway on Tuesday evening. Heather Weintraub and Beverly Wilson met me there. It was a comfort to sit in the back pew and talk to them. Beverly dabbed her eyes. I wondered if she, too, was looking back at her time with Crystal with regret. I wondered if they parted on good terms. People like Crystal are so hard to deal with that you end up wondering if you could have done a better job at holding up your end of the deal. Heather was in her uniform. She was poker-faced, but I knew what she was thinking. We were sure to recognize among Crystal's friends two or three characters who dragged her down. If one of them showed up impaired and said something challenging to Heather, she'd be ready because she wouldn't be surprised. It would be ugly. Nowadays sheriff's deputies sometimes have to work funerals to keep stupid people from acting up and being the center of attention. But we were lucky. A few of Crystal's relatives or friends stood near the casket, which I was relieved to see was closed, but that was it. I didn't see anyone I thought might be her mom or dad. There were two or three funeral sprays. That was it. Someone said Crystal was twenty-seven. She deserved better.

Standing next to the closed casket was Crystal's grandmother. She was dressed nice, all floral, but she looked like hell. She had done her best, but makeup can't cover up exhaustion. I inhaled big before I walked up the aisle to her and introduced myself. Acting like we had never met, I told her Crystal was a sweet girl and I was sorry she lost her. She hugged me and she cried and thanked me. She asked me to pray for her. I haven't done it but I know I should. I motioned for Heather and Beverly to come up. Mrs. Shepherd hugged them too. Beverly told her that Crystal was in a better place. I could never say that, but I was glad Beverly did. It looked like it made Mrs. Shepherd feel better. On the way out of the funeral home Heather said she thought some of the same stuff that got Crystal killed was keeping Mrs. Shepherd propped up. I thought, let her have it.

When we got to the parking lot we told each other that we were glad we had come, for Mrs. Shepherd's sake. It sounded flat. Walk-

ing out of that building into the fall evening air was a relief, but it
felt disorienting. I think the three of us felt a little lost. Cars were
rushing by on Kelly Highway, headed to Wal-Mart or home. The
people in the cars didn't care about Crystal in her casket or poor
Mrs. Shepherd standing next to it. I know the world can't stop when
someone dies, but the thought made me bitter.

It would have been nice to ask Heather to join me at Sweet Bay
for coffee, but it wasn't the right time, or maybe I just didn't want to
enough. We gave each other a nod and weak wave before we got in
our vehicles and drove home in the dusk.

"Better than a warrior"
Mark Burnett

III

Untitled

Of all the rooms in Northside High School's old main building, the one I actively avoided was the teacher's lounge and workroom, but I had copies to run so I made myself go in early on the Monday morning after Thanksgiving. It was the year I got hired. I was getting ready for my second period bunch and was irked at myself for waiting to prep for my classes. My mom, who had enviable self-discipline, complained that she never could win the battle against procrastination. I guess I came by it honestly, as people say.

As usual, I sensed a dismal atmosphere when I stepped through the door, as if the walls were saturated with negative energy from listening to generations of teachers complain about kids. Dishes were piled in the sink. Cheery Thanksgiving decorations stapled to the bulletin board were silently doing their best to counter the depressing vibe. I strolled past one of the long lunch tables like a buffet shopper, inspecting the dried out dessert remnants in cake boxes and pie plates. Much of it was in commercial packaging, but a quarter of a homemade pecan pie in a glass dish looked like it had retained its glory. I picked at it with a plastic knife but the filling had turned into mastic.

I set my cardboard box, my ostentatiously humble briefcase, on a chair next to the copier and found my worksheets. It did not surprise me to see that someone had left a sheet under the lid of the copier. People did it all the time, especially if they got stymied by a paper jam or mysterious electronic mutiny in the guts of the machine, which usually happens when you're in a hurry and the class bell is about to ring. One reason teachers should not have guns at school is that in a rage they'll use them to execute copy machines. What most people do, I suppose, is look at the copy, guess its owner, then put it in one of the mailboxes mounted on the wall or toss it on a work table. This one was covered in notes. I walked back and forth, studying the scribblings, before I dropped the page into my cardboard box and made my copies.

The worksheets were for my troublesome second period class. I had to get ready for them more than my other classes. This meant having worksheets on hand to keep them busy. The worksheets were useful as a threat for when they started talking about the Kardashians or anybody whose nickname starts with Lil'. I'd rather listen to a car alarm. I liked that class, but they were a lot of work. I will never forget them.

It was a small class, just fifteen kids, divided between outspoken, slouching, overgrown white country boys, stereotyped with their long hair, square-toed boots and camo clothes, and, on the other side of the room, assertive black girls, big girls, equally tactless and outspoken and opinionated. I spent the first month keeping them from killing each other.

They were unaware of how much they had in common. You'd think shared traits would unify people, but not this bunch. Maybe they needed someone to point out their similarities, but I wasn't man enough to try. A full account of what they had in common would have to include the first and obvious trait: obesity. These young adults were heifers and yearling bulls. It occurred to me that if they would just cross the gulf, date and marry, they'd be happy with each other, an observation I kept to myself. The messenger would have also to mention their tendency to voice their opinions as if they were unquestionable facts and the enjoyment they took in getting indignant. I was the only person in the room who didn't say exactly what was on his or her mind.

They were a lot of work, but what made it easier was the fact that they were mostly likable, individually, and after a while I learned how to get them to buckle down and learn math. Like me, they were content under a routine. I respected the fact that they were not interested in abstract thinking. They wanted concrete, practical problems and answers. I felt it was my duty to teach them pre-algebra, not inspire them to celebrate mankind's rich diversity. I was courteous but distant. These decisions paid off. Their scorn for each other got to be good-natured and sometimes amusing.

On my way to my classroom, I reflected again about the fact that the women on the faculty did not like me. I hid my concern but it bothered me and I did not know what to do about it. I was approaching thirty, had worked in business and hospital adminis-tration and had never had this problem. It worried me a bit that my boss had to know about it. I nursed my resentment by blaming them, sizing them up as dull, small town bores, but I had to admit that I screwed up and made a bad first impression on them at the beginning of the year. It couldn't be helped now, but time wasn't making things better. Walking down the long halls, past rows of grey lockers, I thought about my family's observation, pointed out to me when I was a boy, that my sense of humor kept me in trouble. Everyone knows email gets people in jams, yet I still got careless.

From day one I chafed under the supervision of our department head, a gal who had the status of curriculum coach. I hid my resentment, but maybe not as skillfully as I thought. Her name was Lynn Freeze. She was a nice looking woman in her late forties, I would guess, and I think she was brainy. She had a folksy way of talking. Listening to her reminded me of Sarah Palin. Her looks and down home speech mannerisms helped hide a talent for calculating that went beyond math. She introduced--imposed, I should say--new methods on our Math department, teaching approaches she described as "awesome" in the day-long meetings before school started. Her methods had some value as an occasional supplement to what I wanted to do, but I had to fake the mild enthusiasm for them I showed in the meetings, mindful that I had been told by the guy who supervised me when I did my practice teaching that they would be quietly dropped and replaced in a year or two. He predicted that whatever came along next would also be described as awesome.

Freeze was adamant about us not deducting points for late work. She said all misbehavior is a result of trauma. I thought she was nuts. Partly, though, I just resented being told what to do. I was cocky. It's the damnedest thing, but lots of coaches aren't good team players, especially when they are young. They are too competitive and opinionated.

So when I got an email from her during my geometry class the first week of school which had a link to an article I was supposed to read before the next department meeting, I agreed to her request, told her so in a way that made me look courteous and cooperative, and hit reply. Then, chuckling, I composed a second email, intending to forward it to my buddy Larry Watson, a coach at Greenwood and the guy I worked under in teacher training. Larry and I mock and scorn educational concepts. They can deserve it, but in truth, it makes us feel righteous. We also share a sense of humor, sometimes regrettably. "Larry, this is what I wanted to tell her. 'We've had public education in this country for a hundred and fifty years and we still can't figure out how to teach math? Yeah, I'll read the stupid article but you gotta have sex with me and it better be good.'"

I was at it again. What was I doing, teaching math in hillbilly Arkansas when I could be making pots of money in the comedy clubs on both coasts? Then I tapped reply again instead of forward. My index finger was coming up from the key when I realized what I had done. I don't know how to describe the sensation that passed through me. Mind nausea? I hated myself. There is no loathing like self-loathing.

I scanned the room. My students were bent over their calculators, trying to work out how to find the arc length and area of circles. Oh, I would have liked to be working on a math problem, the world shut out. I stepped into the hall, closed the door quietly, and with a racing heart, trotted down the hall, trying to outrun an electronic transmission. When I got to her door I could hear Mrs. Freeze talking to her class.

I knocked, not a manly knock, but the weak peck of a pathetic wretch. Every kid in a seat looked at me when she opened the door. I thought about what would happen if just one of them learned what I had done. It would be all over school in a minute. "Can I speak to you out here?" I asked, telling myself not to plead and to be a man.

I backed out of the doorway and looked up and down the hallway. Clearly not happy to be interrupted, she followed me. The hall was empty, a relief. Freeze kept her distance, standing outside our personal space range, frowning. She had to know I was rattled.

"I'm sorry," I said. "Look, I just sent you an email by mistake. It was meant for someone else. It will offend you if you read it. It's dumb and crude. I shouldn't have done it. I thought I was sending it to my friend. Could I ask you please, as a favor, to just delete it and not read it? I swear I did not mean for you to read it and I apologize." I was counting on the fact that women like her often have a gracious side.

Of course I didn't tell her it was about her, about sex with her. She stared over my shoulder then looked directly into my eyes. She did not jump at the chance to rescue me. She was measuring...something. Eye contact was awkward so I looked at her mouth. She had sharp white teeth like a cat and a mole over her lip. Her mouth was full and wide. She was older than me by ten or fifteen years, attractive, with a confident, ladylike demeanor. I'd guess that what she wore came from Dillards, not TJ Maxx.

Our age difference made my suggestion that she have sex with me for reading a stupid math article especially excruciating. A familiar sensation--the same wary feeling I get when I look at a beautiful view from a cliff edge--returned as the seconds ticked.

Finally, she smiled and waved a hand as if to dismiss the issue. "Nothing to worry about, Mr. Wakefield. I haven't seen it yet. We all make mistakes. You better get back to your class." When she closed her door I sagged and exhaled. I thanked God for saving me.

I did accomplish my goal in composing the email. Larry never got it of course, but he hoo-hawed when I told him about my self-inflicted injury. Larry holds unusual opinions, notions that I think come out of the old testament. He left bible college when he was twenty because he didn't fit in. He still doesn't. He's a driven, compulsive guy--before I knew him he ran a marathon a month until he got injured-- but he's a good person and he knows the school business. I told him the story a couple of nights later at Papa's, where we were splitting a pitcher after ordering a pizza. "By the time I got back to my classroom, which had to take less than a minute, I had an email from our principal, who as you know is a woman. She said, "See me when the bell rings. Someone will cover your class.""

Larry waved the cigarette smoke with a menu. "Oh, hell! Well, you still work there. What did she say? Did she write you up?"

"No, she read me the riot act and dismissed me. Told me she was disappointed in me."

"Predictable," Larry said. "Did she use the word 'unacceptable'?'"

"I believe she did. If I screw up again it will be worse was her main message. She was helping with discipline that day. Kids were lined up in the hall waiting to see her. I had to sit outside her office next to some girl who wouldn't give up her cell phone."

"I work with some female teachers who would have laughed off what you did. You got to pick your audience these days. Did you apologize?"

"Sure. I had to. I needed to. I apologized to Mrs. Meyers and to Freeze. She said it was forgotten. Trouble was, she waited till she ratted me out to our principal and the women on the faculty before she got around to forgetting."

"You point that out?"

"What do you think? Hell, no."

"Maybe you shouldn't have told her that sex with her better be good. In fact, it's not too late to make that right. Let her know you never doubted her."

"I don't know how you stay out of trouble, your advice is so bad. Let's get another pitcher and talk about cross-country."

Watson tamped the skoal behind his bottom lip with the tip of his tongue. "Wait a minute. You said those women didn't like you before this. How do you know that?"

"Didn't I tell you that story?" I tried to keep the indignation out of my voice. "The first week of school--the first danged week, mind you-- I went into the lounge at lunch to use the bathroom. Not the main teacher's lounge, but the one in our hall the math people use for lunch. There's just one bathroom in there. Remember, at this time I didn't even know all their names. When I walked out of the bathroom one of those old gals turned around in her chair, her face all red. "Mr. Wakefield!" she said, 'Mr. Wakefield, will you please raise the toilet seat when you use the bathroom?' It was obvious she was a spokesman for the crew."

"Oh hell," Watson said with a snort. "You did screw up."

"As a matter of fact, I did not, by God. I was raised in a matri-archy. A single mom, three sisters, one bathroom. I wouldn't have been fed if I peed on a toilet seat."

What did you say to her?"

"I denied it. She wouldn't believe me. We went back and forth. They were all staring at me when I walked out. I was steamed, you blame me? A couple days later I walked past her coming in the building. She looked at me like I was a rat by a dumpster. So I started using the boy's bathroom on my floor. Along with the wanna be thugs and kids vaping. They don't like me in there but you could pee on the floor and no one would mind."

"Or in a sink," Watson said as he leaned back and frowned. He spit into the styrofoam cup in his fist then took a swig out of his beer glass. "Heathens. So, someone is doing it. Who pees on a toilet seat with a room full of women on the other side of the door? Who uses it beside you? Sounds like a football coach. Heck, blame it on them."

"Yeah, other guys use it, but not very often. Here's what happened. A couple weeks later I was talking to my custodian buddy, Fagan. He was griping about having to fix the commode because the maintenance guys never got around to it. He said he was tired of mopping in there. I asked him what was wrong with it. He said the flush valve leaked. I felt like Sherlock Holmes! I told Fagan my story real quick. After he stopped laughing he told me how it happened. You know these commodes that don't have tanks but have a flush valve lever on a stack? Turns out when the seat is up it leans against the leaking flush valve lever. Water dribbles down the seat. Bingo."

"Makes sense. They go bad because people flush them with their feet. Guys do, anyway. So, you're...what's the word...exonerated. Did you tell that teacher?"

"Nope. She as much as called me a liar. The hell with her. Fagan did say he'd mention it in the lounge."

"I bet your principal heard that story too."

I sighed and shook my head. "That has occurred to me. "I gotta pee. I'll be right back," I said.

"Raise that lid and aim good," Watson said. "Civilization depends on you."

I taught hard all the first day back. Expecting resistance, I made my manner business-like. I knew in a day or two I could joke around a bit, could ask the kids about what was happening in school and what they did over the holiday. A happy surprise, they were in a better mood than I expected and attendance wasn't bad. My troublesome class was a snap. Without much prompting they looked at the bell work I posted on the dry erase board and solved the problems on their Chromebooks while I took roll. Hunched over my document camera in the middle of class, but up front where I could watch them, we worked new problems together. Lights off, I glanced back and forth from the big white screen on the wall to the students. Everybody stayed awake, and if a phone slid out of a pocket I didn't see it. Larry stressed to me during practice teaching that a monotone voice is intolerable for teenagers, so I raised my voice, sped up my words, up and down, while I peppered them with comments and questions as we worked the steps. Five minutes before the bell rang I said, "Good job, guys. Let's quit." The phones flew out.

As I often did, I noticed that the kids in my Pre-AP class learned new math material faster than the kids in regular classes not just because they had more math ability, but emotional stability made it easier for them. They were quieter and calmer than kids in regular classes. Their moods were more stable. Consequently, they were freer to concentrate. I did have some very smart kids. Every semester I had Pre-AP kids who were lots smarter at Math than me. One boy, Manuel Manjarrez, whose father was an engineer at Rheem and whose mother a physician, was such a creative problem solver that I thought he deserved a better teacher. Later I decided that he didn't need a teacher at all. He didn't need me, anyway. I would have liked to set up a rapport with Manuel but he was not a conversationalist. He had little curiosity about others.

When fifth period pre-algebra kids filed in and plopped in their seats, I made adjustments. Three or four of them were repeating the class because they failed it the year before and did not make it up in night school. They knew the material pretty well but wouldn't turn in the work. Getting them busy right away was the key. I took roll before they came in, then made quick corrections for absences and tardies before I sent the account to the attendance secretary. She thanked me every couple of weeks for getting it right and she seemed to like me, a consolation that year. If something has my name on it, I want it done right, even if my boss thinks I'm a yahoo, and crude.

"Good morning, guys. Get your books out." I said, loud enough that the kids up front shook their heads. No one could say they didn't hear me.

"What page?" This from Jonathan Seubold, a blond, muscular boy in a Razorback hoodie, as he reached under his desk.

I ignored the question. I learned that, "Get your books out and open 'em to page twenty-six" was too much information at once, and would not work with these kids. Two minutes into the lesson, the interruptions would start.

"What page we on?"

"Twenty-six," I'd say.

Thirty seconds later, another "What page?"

Then someone would gripe. Kids are no more patient with each other than teachers and less tactful. "He said it two times! Are you stupid?" Two or three others would then pile on. I scanned the room. "Okay. Everyone has their books out? Caron! Caron Roberts! Get your book out. Darren, where's your book? Carlos, put your phone away. You can call your probation officer later." One of my many stock jokes, I use that last line monthly and sometimes get a laugh. "Everybody look at me!" I said, snapping my fingers. "Everybody! Page twenty-six. Got that? No new material here. We're going to review today. You've had it before. It's easy. Let's get started."

I had copies of the textbook pages on the document camera. After we went through the steps I turned the lights on and gave them problems to work on their Chromebooks. I walked around the room, picking up an occasional Chromebook.

"Anthony, you got this stuff? Good. Michael, you told me you learned this last year. Is it coming back? DaVonte, why is your chromebook not charged? Go plug it in. You can work from my desk. Vicki, don't go to sleep on me."

I kicked her chair leg as I walked past her desk. She was struggling to stay awake and she had that washed out, puffy-eyed look. She often walked into my room with a big red spot on her cheek, a sign that her head had been on her desk in her previous class before the bell roused her. I would announce in a booming voice that Vicki Newton had been in the arms of Morpheus, a joke that pleased me because it annoyed her. When I mentioned her problem to one of the counselors, she frowned and said, "Maybe she's working late somewhere. I'll talk to her." I never did find out what the counselor learned, but one day when Vicki was absent I asked her friends about her missing school and sleeping in class.

"Working? Ha! She texted me from the casino last night. That girl never goes home."

"Is anybody stuck?" I asked the class. I straightened up my desk and picked up the wadded paper around the recycling bin. My cardboard box briefcase rested on the floor in front of my file cabinet. I found the sheet of paper which was left on the copier and studied the notes for a minute. In the back, Adin Thompson had his hand up. I walked past him, headed to Angela Martinez's desk. I could see the edge of her round face slowly bobbing above her desk. Resting on her back were braids as thick as dock ropes. She was severely hearing impaired and too shy and gentle to ask for help. She would not wear her hearing aid. It frustrated me that she would not wear her hearing aid, but I could not make myself be forceful with her. She had started the problem but was lost in indecision. I worked half the problem with her, talking to the top of her head, asking her at each step if she agreed that we were doing it right. I'm so loud I have made friends jump when I've yelled at them across a street. Whatever my deficiencies as a teacher, at least Angela could hear me. She glanced at me and smiled when we finished. I felt fortified.

Vicki was upright, but her head rolled around. She was a pretty girl, but too thin. Exhaustion made her look sick and frail. I could fix the problem, I told her father at the first of the year during a planning period phone call. "Let me take her phone away from her," I said. "I'll lock it up. She can get it back when she quits sleeping in class and brings her grades up." I probably shouldn't have made the offer, but he declined anyway.

"No, don't do that," he said. He sounded anxious. "Let me talk to her," he said.

I got halfway back to my desk before I turned back. "What's the matter, Adin?"

"I don't know how to do this. I had my hand up first." His eyes smoldered.

"I'll be right with you," I said. I made slow loops up and down the aisles. "Let me see. Good. Let me see. Terry, open your chromebook. Evan Garcia, did you get it? Good." Not bad, I decided. "Okay, let's quit. There's seven minutes left." I went to Evan's desk, armed with a battle plan. "What don't you understand?"

"None of it. Never mind. The bell's going to ring."

"Yeah, it probably is," I said, in an agreeable voice. "You paid no attention when I explained the lesson. Every time I looked back here you were turned around, trying to talk to the people behind you. You do this every day. Every day you ignore the instructions and then as soon as I give the assignment your hand shoots up and you say you don't know how to work the problems."

"I was listening."

"Nope. You weren't. Another thing, Adin. At the beginning of school I told you guys my pet peeves. One of 'em is I won't stand for people talking about gross stuff, sex stuff, bathroom stuff in my class. This ain't a nasty beer joint on Midland Avenue. I've asked you nice to quit. You know what I'm talking about. No more warnings."

I didn't know what I was going to do about it. My battle plan didn't go that far.

That week, as I ran along the levee trail down by the river, I chewed on the same topic, my work future. People say you only get one chance to make a good first impression and I had blown it at Northside. The brooding started in that first, uncomfortable warm-up mile. It was overcast, cold and windy most of the week. Sunset, which had taken its dreamy time a month ago, often making a showy exit over the Moffett Bottoms, now seemed eager to pounce before I got back to my truck. A west wind lapped the muddy river water against the bank, trapping dirty styrofoam and other trash in the weeds below the running trail, foul stuff the current usually carries downstream to the ocean.

On the phone early that week my oldest sister had asked me in a cheery voice, "How are you liking your job?" I told her I liked my job better than anything I had done before. What I didn't say was for the first time in my career I was alienated from my coworkers and I had a boss who probably wished I would get lost. It would have made me feel uncomfortable to admit that it bothered me. Our mom encouraged us to suffer in silence. Over-sharing was not in our family culture. Then again, maybe I didn't want to tell her about my cute little email trick. While I ran, these thoughts introduced a background issue, one that predated my getting hired as a teacher.

About the time the trail ran up on the levee, my stride would straighten out and get a little more fluid. Relieved to feel less uncomfortable, I tried to raise my gaze from the asphalt six feet in front of me, to notice the lovely sweeping turns the levee made between the box elders and cottonwoods on the flats on each side. Plucked by the cold wind, leaves were spinning out of their crowns, some of them a hundred feet above the floodplain if they were mature cottonwoods. I knew my brooding was keeping me from seeing the beauty in the spectacle. Around that point each day on the trail, I started to wonder if my principal might have a better opinion of me than I thought. I was curious to know what she thought about me. I hoped that she was aware that I was doing a good job. Maybe I was overthinking the issue, was worried about nothing. I constructed imaginary conversations with her which elevated me in her eyes. Then I started to ask myself to what degree did I crave approval and recognition, and if I was over-concerned with what people thought about me. Why was I so worried about it? Did I need petting? Wanting my bosses' approval was something I had never questioned. I thought it was my duty to seek it. Surely no one ever watched me kiss up to a boss. I wondered if, like most people, I hide things from myself. I don't know how you find them.

Only a decision would close the issue. The more I thought about it, the more I decided I needed to strive toward being my own man, to stand above the slings and arrows, by God. This surely was the path to maturity. On Monday and Tuesday I was unsure. Wednesday and Thursday, I was wavering. On Saturday I was convinced. By the time I went on a long run Sunday, including a loop over the Garrison Avenue bridge to the stockyards and back at the end of my standard route, I was convinced. I leaned forward and picked up my pace as I traversed the long slope of the bridge to its rounded crest, where I stopped for a moment, panting in gusts, to look upstream at the Arkansas River lapping in the chilly wind, silty brown water pushing Kansas farm soil toward Fort Smith out of a mighty bend from the Northwest. Semi tractors and trailers behind me clanked as the structure shook. Forget this place, I thought. I could move to Colorado--the river's source. The breeze rocked me back and forth. I felt liberated. God alone would measure my value. The world could kiss my ass. I didn't need its blessing.

It felt great to scorn the judgements of mankind, but the glow only lasted a couple of days. On Wednesday I had an ugly confrontation with a student that got me a spot on Channel Five evening news. I don't think Adin knew I was in the room when he started telling someone--I'm not sure who his audience was--maybe the whole class because everyone could hear him, not just the boys around him in the back of the room--about a recent sexual experience which, to him, was a hoot. I had left the room for hall duty between bells and was stopped in my doorway by the teacher who has the classroom next to mine. She was starting to be friendly to me. We were face to face, having a good conversation, but it got awkward when I--I should say we--started hearing the details of his conquest. I wasn't so embarrassed about hearing him use crude terms for vagina. That was bad enough, but the things he was saying about some poor girl's private parts were disgusting. It would not surprise me if he had named her. My neighbor, who is a teacher, took off for her classroom. I stepped into the room and barked, "Adin, close your mouth!" He looked at me, noted without concern that he had been overheard, then resumed his story in a lower voice, joy in his face. A couple of the boys he was talking to quickly looked away.

The custom is for teachers to stand by our desks and say in a patient voice, "That is not appropriate." Further verbal correction is to be done quietly in the hall. There is the option of filling out a discipline referral form and sending students to the assistant principal's office.

I rushed him. He looked up at me as I narrowed the distance between his desk and mine, unconcerned, until I leaned down and started yelling. Within seconds I was yelling at the part in his hair, not his upturned face.

He looked up once to wail, "You're spitting on me."

"I don't care," I snarled. Thank God that part wasn't on the cell phone video somebody sent to the TV station. Nor was, "You don't have to act like trash."

He said, "I don't have to take this," as he got to his feet and walked out of the room. Before he got out the door I called him a big titty-baby. I had learned that term earlier in the year from my second period class.

"They're going to fire me, aren't they?" I said to Watson when he called me that night to tell me he had just seen me on the ten o'clock news. I was at home stirring a pot of gumbo on the stove. He said the video was jerky and brief but I looked pretty bad. Larry said I wasn't named in the broadcast. Nor had the school district made a comment. He said the TV station probably got the video late. That gave me some time to come up with a defense which would reassure my poor worried mom and keep my bossy sisters at bay, but like the spread of a glorious Fourth of July rocket igniting in the sky, my disdain and aloofness from mankind's judgments fizzled to darkness. Discouragement and embarrassment stayed in the air.

"I don't know, Ed. Don't roll over. They hate to fire people and they don't like lawsuits. That's always in the back of their minds. I won't lie. You looked pretty bad. Like you wanted to strangle him."

"All I did was get loud. Jesus."

"There's this idea floating around that boys are fragile. It is hard to believe people can work around 'em and think that." Watson sighed. "The people who believe that should spend a week in a cabin at summer camp with about twenty boys. What they do to each other for fun can't be described on the evening news."

"Our custodian cleans the counselors' offices. He says boys come in there all mopey because they are fighting with their girlfriends. They want to go home and the school lets them."

"You can ruin a kid if you work hard at it."

"I'll be back in Mrs. Meyers' office tomorrow. Sure as hell." I said.

"What hurt you was the interview with the boy's grandma. She cried for the cameras, which guaranteed they'd run the story. She said you called him trash. She said he struggles in school, and now he doesn't want to go back. It was strange to look at. The grandma blubbered, the reporter talked through an ear to ear grin. It was entertainment, not news. No newspaper would have gotten near it."

"Everyone in Fort Smith is going to think I'm a spitball," I said.

"You better include Northwest Arkansas, but they'll forget in about ten minutes. Noy and I are going to be at Sweet Bay tomorrow at five o'clock. Why don't you meet us? Listen, teachers have gotten away with worse, much worse. Stick your chest out when you walk in there tomorrow."

Convinced that my chosen career had lasted less than four months, I slept badly, but I actually felt pretty peppy when I walked in the building early the next morning. I stayed in my classroom, not wanting to discuss my celebrity status. My troublesome class got me so amused I forgot my troubles for a while. Apparently, in the class before mine, an English class, Wayne Stephens told the teacher there was no way the battle of Thermopylae, 400 BC, could have happened, that the account they were reading was made-up nonsense, because there were no people before Christ's birth, because Christ made us. "Jesus made us," he told the class, and wouldn't back down. Everyone knew that, he insisted. The discussion continued in my class. The girls were still giving him a hard time about, and loving every second. It was clever how they managed to bring it up. No one said anything about my appearance on the news.

Nor did the kids in Adin's class bring it up. I would have liked to know who filmed me, but I knew it was done to share with friends and it wasn't likely that one of my guys sent it to the TV station. Lots of kids probably saw the video, including Adin. He was not in class.

By noon I hadn't heard from my principal. Impulsively, I decided it was time to enlist the help of my curriculum coach, Lynn Freeze. I studied the sheet from my cardboard box one more time. I didn't completely understand what was on the page but I thought my guess was good. Most of what was on the page were numbers. They suggested that curriculum coaches like her were paid stipends in tiers. These were salary supplements for extra duties. Lynn Freeze was not top tier, but all football and basketball coaches were. She was making fifteen hundred dollars a year less than those guys. "I have copies of contracts, PROOF!!" Proof was underlined. Two or three dates from the previous year were linked by arrow to Janet Meyers' name. "No change!! No help!" It wasn't signed, but it said in a margin, "I'm a math specialist! Inequitable...illegal? Ask Joel." A circled sentence stood out: "Suit cannot file till May 30." The last day of school. This was underlined too. I was nervous about being wrong, but it looked like she was leaving our district at the end of the year and intending to sue it. I suspected Joel was an attorney. Our principal would be involved.

At the end of lunch but a few minutes before the bell rang, I knocked on Lynn Freeze's open door and asked to speak to her. She was at her desk, putting on lipstick. I had in my hand the sheet of paper from the copier. "Can I sit down for a second?"

"Yes." I was on my feet, but in her mind she was talking to a man on the ground, wounded. She put her lipstick in her purse and snapped it shut. She dabbed the corner of her mouth with a Kleenex. She took her time doing it.

"I found this on the copier." I slid it to her. "Looks like it's yours. I made a bunch of copies by accident. I just found them in that cardboard box I lug around. I thought you might want it back." Her eyelids widened slightly as she looked at the sheet. "If it isn't yours, sorry to bother you, I can ask around and see whose it is."

"Oh, no. It's mine. Thank you."

The room was quiet. She pressed and rubbed her lips together, sealing in the shiny red wax, as she stared at the back wall. She was measuring me again. The sheet disappeared into a drawer. I stood. The lips popped open. She ran the tip of her tongue over her shiny white teeth. In a brisk voice she said, "You say you made copies?"

"Yeah, but I recycled them. I think that's the only one." I dragged my gaze from her mouth to her eyes.

"Thank you, Mr. Wakefield," Her voice was quiet and confidential. "By the way, I hear you're doing an awesome job in the classroom. Awesome."

"Thanks," I said. "If you would mention that to our boss I'd appreciate it."

"I'd be glad to," she said. "Glad to."

I walked into Sweet Bay, which Larry calls a secular bar, at 5:30, dusk already, and saw patrons in corduroy and scarves, snuggling up to their iPads and laptops, their conversation a murmur. No one stared at a ball game. Sweet Bay is not as much fun as Papa's, but I do like it that the windows aren't covered from floor to ceiling. The light fixtures and the wallpaper remind me of being in the lobby of a dermatologist's office. Unlike Papa's, the air is breathable. At the counter I got a regular coffee, and, needing a snack--a scone. Larry and his girlfriend Noy were sitting at a table under a forgettable painting of flowers in a vase, an empty chair waiting. "Sorry I'm late. I just left my principal's office," I said.

"Hey, man, how did it go?" It wasn't a pro forma question. He really wanted to know. It is a mighty good feeling to have an ally.

"I got the idea that she thinks they'll get rid of me," I said. "She said she didn't know that for sure and she didn't come right out and say it. And I have to admit, she made it easier on me, the conversation I mean, than I thought it might be. Sabaidee, Noy, how are you?" I said, using the Laotian greeting in a cheery voice. I smiled at them, showing the world I wasn't a beat down puppy.

"I'm good, thanks. Sabaidee." It is easy to smile at Noy. She's a beautiful Laotian girl, a little heavy, but her face is a nice composition of features. I'd want to go to a botany text if I had to describe her skin and eyes and mouth. Heck yeah, I envied my pal.

On the other hand, Larry's mug, with his bony chin jutting out under his thin horizontal lips, and those level forehead skin folds when he raised his straight brows, suggests geology. Layer and deposition, permanence. Noy's features look delicate, but consistent with looks being deceiving, she will be as beautiful as a flower into old age. Poor guy, around retirement Larry will resemble a limestone bluff in the Ozarks. Larry and Noy are compatible, not in interests, but in values, he says. He says that his being an absolutist who rejects a lot of grey area doesn't bother her, because she's Asian. She's a pharmacist. Her dad pastors a Laotian Baptist church. Larry doesn't like his theology, but he says about her family, with admiration, "They don't flinch."

"I did get a little testy with her. She said Adin was struggling. I took issue with that."

Larry looked at Noy. "All students who are failing or who have discipline problems are labeled as struggling. It's nonsense. They aren't struggling, most of them. Struggling implies effort."

"Then she wanted to know exactly what Adin said and I wouldn't tell her. I said she could find out from one of the other students. I told her to ask a girl. She took that to mean that I thought she was some kind of frail Victorian. It irritated her. By the way, I'm not going to say it in front of you, either, Noy."

"I don't need to hear it," Noy said. "Or want to. Forgive me for not being sophisticated."

"She said it would be hard for me to defend my actions if I refused to say what happened."

Larry leaned back and shook his head. "She's got a point there, Ed."

"I did tell her I gave him several warnings. I said I might end up writing down what he said in a discipline form. I wouldn't mind that, but I want to see what admin is going to do. I told her if they fire me then what I do will be up to my attorney."

"First salvo in the battle. Good." He tilted his head. "Maybe by refusing to say the words it puts an emphasis, a focus on what was said, because I assure you they'll want to forget about what he said and make a big deal about what you did."

"I held my temper, didn't get sarcastic, kept the tone courteous like you advised. Really, the conversation was friendly. I think she appreciated that."

"What else?"

"I told her if I get fired, the words would be said by someone at admin in a courtroom. If I have to say it they'll have to say it."

"Okay, I don't know how helpful that is, but maybe."

"She scolded me for not going through the steps. I pushed back, but I gave a little ground. I said I was sorry that the whole thing happened and that she had to get involved and I knew she had better things to do. But I said, 'Let's be honest. If I wrote him up he'd get in- or out-of-school suspension. Both are a vacation. A reward. "

"Yep. He'd sleep during in-school suspension. If you send them home they play video games all day."

I told her I didn't blame her for that, told her I knew it wasn't her doing, that I figured she might do things differently if she had her druthers.

"Please finish this scone, someone."

"That's probably true." Larry popped the rest of the scone in his mouth, a thoughtful look on his face as he chewed. I noticed his lower lip was not crowded with his beloved Wintergreen. "I hear she's a good principal."

"I hear that too," I said. "I told her I regretted her not knowing that I was trying hard to be a good teacher, and she said she heard I was doing an awesome job. Maybe she'll go to bat for me."

"Guys who don't respect women have a weird contempt for female private body parts," Noy said in a firm voice. "It's strange and sick. In parts of the world women are still forced to isolate when they are menstruating. How did that come about?"

"They're considered unclean," Larry said.

Noy stared trance-like at a distant point past us, then with a startled look, ducked her face into her elbow sleeve, sneezing with a shrill "PEEK!" like a bird. She dabbed her nose with the napkin Larry handed her and said, "My father heard my brother refer to someone as a pussy one time because he thought the guy was weak. This was in the car. My dad got all over him, not because the word was crude, but because it made him mad to hear weakness associated with a word that mostly means...well not a cat, but something else."

"I read about a college basketball coach who used to put a tampon in his player's lockers when he was not happy with their performance," Larry said.

"Well, it's the Christmas season," Noy said. "So let me tell you what else my father said. He told us a woman's private body parts are sacred and a man's aren't. He said Israel is sacred because God chose it as the place where Jesus was born. Then Bethlehem, then the manger, then Mary's womb. Down the line. All sacred. Consecrated." Noy shook her head. "It upsets my mom when he talks about this stuff. She's a Victorian, a Lao Victorian."

"Ed, I hope you survive to teach another day. I hope you can break into coaching next Fall."

"I appreciate that, Coach," I said.

"I bet you'll never see that kid again. They'll send him to alternative school. He'll fit in there. If you don't hear from the admin in a day or two you're safe, unless the parent sues. In that case, you're overboard. Oh, they might put a reprimand letter in your file. Who cares? I tell ya, though, you're never going to get along with those women till you quit peeing on the toilet seat in their bathroom."

"What?" Noy said, alarm in her voice.

"He'll explain later," I told her as I stood up to leave. "He'd better. I don't need any more women thinking I'm foul."

A one sentence text from Noy arrived Sunday evening. It read, "He who is slow to anger is better than a warrior, and he who controls his temper is greater than one who captures a city." Proverbs 16:32. It was a lash on my back and I deserved it.

Before the end of the week my principal told me, in passing, that a reprimand would be placed in my file, that I needed to come by her office and sign it. It made me mad, but I kept my mouth shut, figuring I better eat what was on my plate. When I went to her office the next day she wasn't there. I did not go back and she never brought it up. At the end of the year a couple of my co-workers retired. The young female teachers who came up changed the personality of the department.

Not that I fantasized about her, or missed her, but for a while I kept a secret curiosity about what became of Lynn Freeze, a matter of lingering resentment, I told myself. I did admit to myself that she surely never had a backwards thought about me.

It bothers me that I can't say what became of any of those kids I taught my first year, Travis and Wayne and Toya and LaKeisha and the rest. Not one. It's curious how people vanish. It comforts me to say it was some time until my mouth got me in trouble again.

"The Home of the Blind Salamander"
Mark Burnett

IV

Wakefield & The Killer Hoes

The checker at the Ten Box store on Grand, a friendly black woman about my age who knew me by sight, scanned the last of my groceries and told me the total. I leaned toward her and said in a quiet voice, "I'm paying for hers, too," nodding to the customer following me, a young woman lifting items out of her little basket onto the conveyor.

I had dawdled, then angled my cart in ahead of her, having spotted her as she pulled items out of the freezers on the frozen food aisle, a good place to look her up and down. I stared at her through a steamy glass door to make sure. Yep, Renee. AKA Ray Ray. The purple streak at the back of her head, a new touch, looked like it was done with a Sharpie marker, but she wasn't dressed badly, in jeans, flats and a blue sweatshirt with a U of A emblem. We almost brushed shoulders when she pushed her cart past mine. I held my breath as she gave me an uncomprehending glance. Her square shoulders were pulled back, her movements graceful. I wondered where she picked that up.

It took me a minute to arrange my sacks of groceries in my cart. By the time I was ready to shove off she was pulling cash out of her jeans pocket. The smiling cashier said, "He already paid for it."

Renee gave me a blank stare. She frowned and squinted at me, started to speak, then recognition bloomed. It took her a moment to recognize me, the guy she was on top of, naked, four months ago, on my living room couch with the lights on. Sheesh. She looked startled and afraid. I said, "It's okay, Renee," as she cringed. "It's all right." The checker's smile was frozen. She didn't like it.

Renee started to babble about her sister. Nope. I turned my back. Buying her a few groceries was one thing. Not that I expected or wanted gratitude. I pushed my cart through the big glass doors out to the littered parking lot, wondering again if what I did was right. It's what you do after every encounter with the Renees of the world.

Years back my pals and I were on a Buffalo River gravel bar, that pretty stretch below Woolum with the towering bluffs and gravel bars that sweep around the bends in the river. Our coolers and tents and lawn chairs were strategically placed around the camp by one of the more particular members of the party. Merrick was at the camp kitchen we had set up on an overturned canoe, cleaning what little was left over from a chicken pot pie I had prepared in a dutch oven. Narisi lugged firewood from his boat to a pile beside the fire, across from where I sat in my retro lawn chair with the nylon weave and aluminum tubes. I had taken a Motrin and a THC-infused gummy. I pop these into my mouth only rarely and don't fear them, but experience has taught me to regard the three ounces of my beloved Macallan Scotch melting the four ice cubes in the metal coffee mug in my hand as a serpent which will strike my heel if I get careless.

It had been a fine day, the sky a blue you see on old tiles. The mountain range of clouds which had assembled all afternoon, in celestial not geologic time, wandered off, restless to visit someplace else, as we beached our boats. There's no evidence for reincarnation in Christian scripture, but if it exists, I want to come back as a cloud.

Late Autumn in Arkansas means terrific weather and sometimes showy foliage but low water; we did scrape in the shallows some, but a so-called "too low to float" trip means fewer folks and can take on a peaceful, quiet character, if a little more work. Avoiding the shallows makes you read the water. We were in separate boats, paddling apart from each other much of the day. I stared at the sky and scenery, my avocation being a "cloud inspector," to steal Thoreau's phrase. Up ahead, Bob yakked with the folks floating by. It is his nature to be a serial friend maker. At dinner he recounted a conversation with a young Mormon couple from Salt Lake. His description of them was so uplifting I wished they were with us. His encounter did not surprise me. It is a cliche to say that you meet the nicest people on the trails and rivers. Only a snob would refuse to say it.

Pulling fish out of the water has never appealed to me, despite decades of floating lakes and streams, but I could read the union of contentment and silent concentration on Narisi's face and saw it as a fine thing. Steve never married but he has multiple lovely mistresses, one being his ties and fly rod kit. I envied him as he cast into the deep pools.

The sunrise and sunset tables said a three quarter moon would rise at 10:48. Moonlight would reveal the broad bluff face across the river, dim, but spooky and magical, especially in the time of morning Sinatra called the wee hours. A gleam would reflect off the water till the moon set.

My pals worked in the news business. We would stay up late and talk about all kinds of stuff.

Then Bob said from the kitchen, "I heard Fort Smith cops arrested the person who murdered that retired teacher. Did y'all hear that?"

I did not know about the arrest, but the murder, a brutal beating that left blood all over the victim's apartment, was a big news item and had happened three blocks from my house, so I was curious about it. It had happened just a few days ago.

Steve said, "They arrested a young woman while she was driving the murdered guy's car. They caught her outside a drug house out by the fairgrounds. Ed, you may remember her. A Savannah Miller. She went to Northside."

Indeed I did. I suspected we were talking about the girl I remembered. It gave me a cold feeling.

"You knew that teacher, didn't you, Ed?" Bob said.

"I met him. Didn't know him. He coached around here a long time ago. I guess he lived alone, didn't get out much."

"Someone she knew lived next to him," Bob said. "A relative, maybe, so she got to know him. She told the cops a couple of stories. One was he loaned her the car. Another was that she got sexually involved with him and he gave her money but she didn't kill him. Then she admitted that she stole his car."

"I had her in class, if it's the same one," I said. "Nice kid, quiet. Damn."

"I bet you a no-good boyfriend was involved." Bob said. "Women don't beat people to death. They didn't used to, anyway. I'm leaving the coffee out. It's ready. Whoever gets up first can start it."

The THC in the gummy was coming on, slow but strong. The dosage may have been a little heavy that night. Pot works for me on just two occasions, when I listen to music and clean my house, a barely tolerable chore that weed makes pleasant, and sitting around a campfire late, the fewer the folks around the better. It would have been better to not be under the influence when I heard the news about Savannah. My mind acted like a Rubik's cube, scrambling, one different rotating thought per colored square succeeding another. It wasn't pleasant. Unimpaired, I would have tired of it. I would have pushed the news aside and joined my buddies as they talked about baseball, or travel, or investing money, anything but the image of a rage filled young woman I once knew, standing over a cowering, blood-spattered old man. The THC fed my uneasiness as I waded deeper into the scene. Nearly every discrete thought I had about her was sandwiched by suspicion that she must be guilty and after that thought flew off, certainty that she could not have been more than an accomplice. I remembered that I did not know her well. That thought scrambled to the memory of her sitting near the front of my classroom, over by the shelves and tall windows. She was a quiet girl. She was a brunette of medium height, well-groomed, with a pad of flesh at the inside corner of her eyes that made me wonder if she had Asian blood. She looked wholesome. I had trouble with one of her quirks. She talked like she was black. Sometimes white kids do that. I am impatient with this phony sounding nonsense. I always saw it as a sign of a poorly adjusted kid. She got very angry when I teased her about it. Scramble again. She couldn't have done it. Scramble. Come on, she was caught in his car. Fat chance she was innocent. Scramble again. She told the girl who sat next to her that the only guys she liked were thuggy. She probably did it. Maybe the poor old man was just trying to help her. Scramble back to her innocence. Her boyfriend did it and she won't rat him out. She is young, foolish, headstrong, wasn't raised right, tragically damaged. Scramble.

She got to my class earlier than most kids. We rarely talked, but one day when my room was still mostly empty, she said, "Mr. Wakefield, is your wife classy?" She looked troubled. What a question. No student ever asked me anything like it.

I did not tell her I was divorced. I said, "Yeah, she is, Savannah. She's not stuck up, but she has a lot of self-respect." I watched her frown but she didn't say anything else. It was as if she knew there was not much chance that she was going to be classy, but it was still a possibility. Some people think that the main psychological task teenagers have to work on is discovering their identities. This involves trying on roles to see if they fit. I guessed that she was thinking about trying one on, but what did I know about her? It was like she picked up a dress, looked at it, decided she'd never wear it, and hung it back on the rack. Later, when I learned how low class her family was, this got clearer.

I peered into the coals, self conscious about Steve and Bob having lively, wholesome conversations without me. The impulse to help Savannah, brief but intense like the other thoughts in this messy progression, caused a cascade of suspicious self-warnings along the line of her manipulating me and how she might do it. Everyone knows that running scams is a cottage industry in jails. She told the cops she was sexually involved with her victim. All she would remember about me, if she remembered me at all, was that I was a teacher and an old guy in her eyes, like the poor man she killed. I would never let her do that to me. Male pride would not let me consider her a physical threat, but she might try to find a way to exploit me. I did not want to look back and see that I had given her the opportunity. I needed to think about keeping her at a distance. I wondered, idly I hope, if she was still pretty. A voice--a loud voice-- told me to stay away from her.

I can't blame the cannabis for the decisions I eventually made, but learning about Savannah when I was elevated from the pot and the whiskey may have set in motion a subtle process that nudged me toward over-thinking and indecision, a condition that possibly lingered around the issue as my subconscious worked on it. I am convinced that our subconscious works on problems. My behavior never got shameful, but any time a guy who generally stays out of trouble, who hasn't even had a traffic citation in years, gets involved with a murderer and her cutthroat family he ought to think about the forces that influenced his decision making. The idea that people are presumed innocent till proven guilty didn't help me much, either. It was a square on the Rubik's cube which kept turning up. It felt like a burden. Continuing the argument that none of this was my fault, which I admit sounds pretty chicken-shit, I can say that I did get commanded by divine authority to get involved in a bad situation. This is still tough to reconcile. Talk about over-thinking this issue, I have wondered if an advisory board on the matter should have included a theologian. What to think of that will be another rubik cube square which can spoil a future marijuana experience, if I let it.

A week or so after the float trip I attended Sunday services at Saint Boniface Church. I love that old brick pile. The high ceiling and gothic arches give me a sense of satisfaction as I find a place in one of the long pews, usually in the back, where it pleases me to think that those in most need of salvation sit. Even though the congregation is increasingly composed of Mexican families, for me the old Germanic atmosphere lingers, enough to suggest that serious business goes on there, that this is not Target or Academy Sports. I turned around in my seat to study the forbidding stained glass image of Boniface, the English saint who ministered to the German tribes, being martyred by a barbarian chief. I had already glanced at the window as I walked up the front steps to the entrance. It was not lost on me that the scene, lurid and drenched with color when the sunlight hits it right, and as big as a billboard, depicted a savage murder, that congregants enter the church under a scene of a man murdered while doing good deeds.

In the last decade or so it has almost become predictable that the priest will urge us in his sermon to reach out to others, to help the less fortunate, the marginalized, the poor, the broken. I expect in every sermon to be told to not judge others who are different, even if that message does not have a close connection to the gospel reading for the week. If I'm being honest with myself, judging others who are not like me has not been one of my big failings, nor do I often see it in others, yet it seems that this issue gets more attention than the seven deadly sins: lust, greed, gluttony and sloth, wrath, envy and pride, all of which have ganged up on me from time to time. So of course I heard it again that Sunday from Father Mario, from the pulpit, with no mention that helping the downtrodden gets tricky, complicated, or can be counter-productive, and can get you used and even killed by one of the downtrodden that you are reaching out to, like Boniface and maybe the old retired coach beat to death a few blocks from my house.

Sebastian County Jail has an online Care Package Program. Anonymously, I activated an account for Savannah and put forty bucks on it for stuff like toothpaste and shampoo. Done, I thought. One evening at George's while I was sitting at a big table, someone who was friends with the murdered man's niece told the table that Savannah had racked up several discipline violations in jail, that she got in fights with the other prisoners, that she had older sisters who were employees in the world's oldest profession. More evidence that she was guilty. What I heard about Savannah in the restaurant that evening spiked the notion of a jail visit.

Weeks passed. I thought I might hear that she wised up and told a detective about an accomplice, some low-life guy who was already taking up with another foolish doormat of a girlfriend, but it didn't happen. Then one morning I read in the Southwest Times Record that she had been convicted for the murder and earned a forty year prison sentence. You got the idea from the news article that the court thought she was guilty as sin. There wasn't much else I could do for her, but I was safe from involvement. I'd be dead and forgotten when she got out of prison. Time ran on, as it does. A couple of years later I put another forty bucks on her toiletries account and sent her a Christmas card, addressed to her new home at the

McPherson Unit of the Arkansas Department of Corrections. Not interested in being her pen pal, I told her I did not like to write letters but I wanted her to know that I remembered her as a nice person and a smart girl and I said something about redemption and grace and prayer. I did not let her know that I had put the money on her account. I scanned what I wrote a couple of times. It looked so lame I left the envelope on my mantle for a few days before I sent it. It was just a card. I did not have a good reason to put my return address on it but I did.

During the next three or four years I confined my efforts at being a compassionate person to sending occasional small donations to organizations like the Fort Smith History Museum, environmental groups and the local animal shelter. Meagre offerings they were, but safe bets. Otherwise I didn't reach out to the downtrodden. In truth, there are a couple of categories of disadvantaged people which I regard with suspicion. This troubles me. Anyway, I didn't think much about Savannah Miller.

She re-entered my life at the end of flu season, or I should say her agents did, the timing a coincidence I pondered for sometime. I had been feeling peculiar for a day or two. Since getting annual flu shots for several years, I had not been down with that bug or even had a cold, and it being the end of the season, with little of either around, so I thought, it did not occur to me that I was going to get sick. One morning, at work, I knew something was wrong. During my third period class I felt uncomfortable and listless with a bewildering overlay of depression. I had awareness enough to know I had done a poor job teaching. When the bell rang I left my room for hall duty, as usual, joining Becky Nageland, the teacher who mostly coaches girl's basketball and who has the classroom next to mine. We have several conversations each day which last three minutes. It was a relief to lean against the wall.

"What's wrong with you?" she said, looking down at me.

"Nothin."

"Are you sick?"

"I don't know," I said. " I don't feel right."

Becky is forceful and blunt. She's a bit over six feet one inches tall and a former college basketball player. Her college team didn't lose many games. When I first met her, she limped into my room to introduce herself. She laughed as she explained that her podiatrist had just performed a surgery on her toes, damaged from getting her feet stomped on under a basketball goal during a decade of playing. What that doc did to her sounded like a veterinary procedure, but Becky is one of those types who sneers at pain and is incapable of self-pity. I wasn't about to go on about my symptoms.

I'm attracted to her, but even if she were single, I'd probably pass, freely admitting that she's too much woman for me. Her six foot six inch husband knows the banter between Becky and me gets outrageous. He's a good fellow. Early in our friendship I was careful to find out if he was jealous or possessive. If he was, I would have changed my behavior, not that she would hers. When she was pregnant I wisecracked once or twice about how a particular zone of her anatomy in the higher altitudes was swelling before I came to my senses and told myself to keep my mouth shut. She says pretty much whatever she wants about me.

One time I said to her, "Coach, if we were both single and I was younger, would I have a chance with you?"

"No. Get lost."

"Well, I don't usually ask this," I said, "but will you tell me why?"

"Yeah, you're too short. Scram."

She placed her hand on my forehead. Her palm felt cool against my skull. "You're burning up, Wakefield." Even female coaches use last names. "You need to go home."

We had a substitute teacher in the building who wasn't being used. An assistant principal brought her to my classroom a few minutes later. "Coach Nageland says you're sick. Why don't you go home?" It was a command with a question mark.

I went by Available Medical Care on the way home. Like most people who walk in the place, what I mostly was after was a prescription. I didn't care so much about the diagnosis as getting symptom relief. Wanting so badly to be at home in bed in my old house on Clifton Court, I figured I'd be out of there in an hour or two. My heart fell when I saw that the waiting room was full, every chair occupied by an exhausted looking mom rocking a pitiful child. Women were sitting on the floor, their backs to the walls, crying kids spread out on blankets. I got out of there about three slow hours later with a prescription for Tamiflu in my hand, having been told that an evil late season flu virus was spreading, making people very sick. I went straight home and didn't get out of bed except to stagger to the bathroom until mid-morning the next day. Looking at myself in the mirror was humbling.

Becky called me. "Are you feeling better?"

"No. I'm not." I was burning up. "I hope you don't get what I got. I've never been this sick."

"What can I do for you?" she asked.

"Well, I hate to ask you, but I need a prescription filled. Can you go by Coleman Pharmacy and get it for me? They phoned it in."

"Sure, but it'll have to be after basketball practice and I pick my kids up."

I told her that was fine. I told her I'd leave the back door unlocked in case I was conked out and she could leave the medicine on my kitchen table. I wanted to know how my sub did but I couldn't hold on to the thought. I ate half a bowl of cereal at the counter in my kitchen until I got the twirlies and knew I better get back in bed. I made it there in stages. Before I got out of the kitchen I felt so weak I had to lower myself to the linoleum floor where I stared stupidly at the baseboard, shivering from chills, till I got the strength to get up. Halfway across the dining room I lowered myself to the carpet, spent again already. Conflict and self pity ebbed and surged in me. No one could know how sick I was. I was resentful at the accusation that men are melodramatic about sickness symptoms. I wanted to be manly and downplay my symptoms but I was shocked at how bad I felt.

Sleep, deep blessed sleep, until the damned doorbell rang several times. I got a robe from my closet and walked slowly through my living room to my front door. I fought the lock and dead bolt until I cursed. A figure at the screen door which opened onto my porch looked through the screen, her hands cupped around her face. It irritated me to see that it wasn't Becky with my Tamiflu. A strange young woman stood on the top step. I didn't find out just how strange she was till later. There wasn't a vehicle in the driveway.

I didn't know if it was an hour after sunset or three a.m. My bones were aching and my feet were freezing. Not a lot about her looks registered, but I know she was a lanky blond. She talked in a burst.

"Mr. Wakefield my sister's lawyer filed a motion to get her conviction overturned and get her a new trial and I'm asking you to write a letter to the court which says she is a good person cause some new stuff has come out and I thank you so much for what you've done for her...."

"Wait. How am I supposed to know who your sister is?" It took effort to be that nice.

She looked bewildered. She tossed her hair, wagged her chin and said, " My sister is Savannah Miller I'm sorry I promise you I'm not asking you for money my sister is a good girl and everyone has turned their back on her I'm her sister Renee. Her lawyer filed a motion to get her conviction overturned and get her a new trial and I'm asking you to write a letter to ..."

"I'm sick. I can't talk right now. Come back in a few days." I turned around at the door before I thought better. "Write your phone number down and leave it in my mailbox." She kept it up as I walked away. I hadn't said I'd help her, but the way she talked, it would be the greatest thing any human being had ever done for another. She continued to thank me in a pleading voice as I closed the door. I guess she walked home.

I lay on the couch with a folded afghan over me, staring past the coffee table at the little wall of blue flame throbbing in the gas fireplace logs. My eyelids rose and fell as I slipped in and out of sleep, but disturbing dreams, rapid-paced and nonsensical, kept me near the surface of wakefulness. The doorbell rang again, with rapid knocks. Finally, Becky with the Tamiflu. I thought.

As soon as I opened the front door, skinny Renee chest-bumped me, pushing me back. Another woman, also blond but bigger, chattered as she followed Renee. She was taller than Renee, had a linebacker torso over pipestem legs. She turned, closed the door, fought with the lock, gave it up, turned and said, "Sugar, Ray-Ray says you're sick. You poor baby. We gonna make you feel good."

"Party time," Renee said in a happy voice as she put her hands on my chest and pushed me back. She pronounced it like potty.

The bigger girl pulled on my housecoat. I tried to shove Renee's hands away. I figured they were there to rob me. "What do you want?" I said. "What do you want?" I struggled, but we stumbled past the back of the couch in an awkward three person dance, Renee pushing, the other behind me pulling on my robe.

"Now you be nice, old man. We don't want to have to get rough with you," Renee said.

They got me to the narrow space between my couch and coffee table. The struggle drained me. I was nauseated and my movements were feeble. The big girl plopped in a chair at the end of the couch, tapping at her phone while Renee pulled down my boxer shorts. My housecoat was pulled behind my back, one arm still in the sleeve. Renee pushed me down on the couch. My boxers ended up around my ankles. She stood between my feet, kicked off her jeans, pulled her long sleeved T-shirt over her head, lay them on the coffee table. No bra, no panties. She straddled me, wiggling into place. The girl with the pleading voice I had talked to earlier on the porch, filled with a tender concern for her sister, was now auditioning for a porn actress role. Confident in her talent, she made hunching motions against my belly with her hips while big girl took photos of us. She was trying to mimic passion but the expressions on her face were disgusting. She was open mouthed and her eyes were slits. She panted like a little dog on a hot day. She had put on makeup for the performance. Chrome colored eyeliner went past her eyes to a tapered point. I could see dark roots next to her skull. An unfinished, poorly drawn tattoo of Tweety Bird giving the finger ran from her collar bone down to her breast.

I wasn't just weak and nauseated. My arm pinned behind my back in the robe sleeve hurt like hell. She tried to pull my free hand up to her breast but I wouldn't do it. I tried to turn my face away from Big Girl and her phone, but Renee grabbed my chin, forcing me to face her. That was the extent of my resistance. She rotated to sit sideways on my lap, her arm clasped around my neck, her knees apart, a crowning moment in her performance. I don't know if I ever felt such rage.

"Be nice, now, old man. If you be good we won't have to hurt you. We can get rough, honey. We can get real rough."

"Ray Ray, don't say no more," the big girl said.

The action stopped. Ray Ray frowned and turned her head. Big Girl looked up from her phone. I followed their eyes. Becky stood in the doorway between the dining room and living room. She was wearing a buttoned up red cardigan tied at the waist, the hem circling her knees. She carried a white sack in both hands at her waist.

She was poised and pokerfaced, considering what she was looking at.

"Uh, coach..." she said.

I was afraid she'd turn and leave. I rallied. "Get her off me, Becky. They broke in. Get that phone. Get that damned phone."

"What is going on?"

"They broke in. Get that phone."

"You ain't getting my phone," Big Girl said.

Becky looked a little uncertain but she backed me as she approached the couch. "Girls, put your phones on the coffee table." It was polite, teacher talk. It saves face for a kid who has to give up their phone to not have to hand it to an adult, makes it more likely they'll give it up.

Renee hopped off me, turned and started getting into her jeans. She bounced on one foot, her narrow white ass in my face. Big Girl stood. Renee pulled her shirt over her head.

"We got what we want. Let's go," she said.

The couch, the fireplace mantle and my two wing-backed chairs make a three sided box. The coffee table fills most of the middle. The way out led past Becky.

"Girls, put your phones on the coffee table." She looked down at me. I was trying to cover myself.

"Coach, who are these goofballs?"

"I don't know. Blackmailers, I guess." I said.

My guests turned into bobcats. Renee got to Becky first, her fists windmilling, rage on her face. "Stupid bitch," she hissed. Big Girl almost ran over her trying to get ahead of her.

Becky turned into a center under the net. She could have whipped those two while she dribbled a basketball. She body slammed Renee into the mantle, forcing her forearm under her chin, her open hand out to her side to block Big Girl's charge. She pushed off Renee, glided sideways to her left, putting her elbow in

Big Girl's face and at the same time her hip and waist rammed into Big Girl's round belly. Big Girl landed on my coffee table with a crash, scattering my books, magazines, and my brass candle holder. Becky returned to Renee. She grabbed Renee's hair and jerked her head back and forth. "Will...you...put...your...phone...on...the...coffee...table." Each word got a jerk. Renee pulled her phone out of her back pocket, crying "Ow...Ow...Ow" as she threw it to the floor. Becky let her go. Big Girl rolled off the coffee table onto the floor with a thud. She got up slowly, pulled her phone out of her pocket and dropped it on the table.

"Do we call the cops?" Becky said.

I couldn't think. What a decision. "Not now," I said. I was done. "Let 'em go.'"

"Get out of here. Next time I won't be so nice," Becky said as the two veered around her.

The crew went by her and circled the couch in a trot but jerked to a stop when they saw Jeff Nageland filling the front doorway. One of his big hands held a tall styrofoam container. The other was wrapped around a six pack of drinks. I don't know how long he had been there but he stared at Becky for a second and finally shook his head, as if to say, "What am I gonna do with her?" The girls slipped around him like water around a boulder. I could hear them cursing Becky a blue streak out on the porch. I guess they walked home.

"We brought you chicken noodle soup from Paul's Meat Market and some Gatorade," he told me.

"I better get in bed," I said to him.

Until those two harpies forced their way into my house when I was in a pathetic state I never ever felt the temptation to hit a girl or woman, not even when I had arguments with them that left me feeling like I burned brain cells. So it disgusted me when I caught myself daydreaming about slapping and cursing them like they were animals as they fled my living room. For a while I stayed out of there.

It was not possible to sit on my couch and sort my mail or read the Arkansas Democrat Gazette on my iPad without remembering the incident. A hard part was admitting that I was ashamed. I felt tainted by feelings of worthlessness I couldn't drive away. Telling myself that I hadn't done anything wrong didn't help. I wanted to call Becky and ask her to not tell anyone about what happened, but it seemed like a weak thing to do and I hated to ask her for further help, knowing she would never blab about a friend's embarrassing situation anyway. If the story got out, it would race through my family and friends. Ironically, I was concerned that my ex-wife, who kept her ear to the ground for what went on in Fort Smith, would think that I was in some kind of trashy sex scandal. At that time I still wanted to think that she regretted our breakup. So I tidied up the National Geographics on my coffee table, straightened the brass candle holder and threw away their phones after beating the hell out of them with a hammer in my garage, swinging between bouts of patient acceptance over what happened and angry resistance every time the memory returned.

At the time it seemed just like uncomplicated resentment. Why not? Common criminals probably, they had forced their way into my house. Later I wondered if the fretting meant that there was a debate going on deep in my mind. Not a lot about the college psychology course I took years ago resonated with me, but I do remember drawing a mental picture when I first learned about the subconscious that is so vivid I keep it with me. I picture in my case a cave with deep and winding passages, unexplored and inaccessible, where sunlight is alien. My thoughts which live down there have as their counterparts blind salamanders and odd cave crayfish. It doesn't take an insightful person, which I probably am not, to know that those critters need to be protected from contamination--and left alone.

My instructions are to first ask Providence for help in all things but as usual I skipped that and tried to reason away my resentment. Those girls, or women (I did not know what to call them), had not hurt me physically nor had they gone out the door with my money or stuff. Many people go through much worse. My experience taught me nothing about what victims of real sexual assault go through. It made me angry to think that such things happen.

Assistance can come in unexpected times and places. Weeks later a reconciliation moment occurred when Narisi and I were shuttling his truck on War Eagle Creek, having already dropped our kayaks at the put-in place, where Bob sat in a lawn chair on the gravel bar, guarding our stuff while he drank a beer and read a newspaper. A float on a pretty day is a wholesome activity, fertile ground for forgiveness seed. As we drove back to Withrow Springs on an unpaved country road with no houses, a big, mottled cur with a collar loped toward us on a curve, trotting purposefully ahead, chin up, gait confident.

"He's on his way home," Narisi said. "Probably had a great time today getting in trouble."

This small talk did not particularly register until later, when we saw two more dogs in the brush and litter by the side of the road. They were cute little guys, litter mates maybe, long-legged with dirty, curly white hair. Steve slowed to give them a look. "Strays," he said. "Disgusting. How can people do that?"

"How do you know they're strays?"

"Look how they act." The dogs crouched in the brush, their spines curved. They stared at us warily. "They're afraid."

A woman I worked with, a therapy dog trainer, convinced me that dogs have a wider set of emotions than I ever suspected, so it was easy for me to believe that I saw not just fear in the eyes of those little mutts, but shame.

"Dogs who have been dumped are hard to rescue. If you get out of your car and throw food at them and call to them in a kind voice they slink away." He looked at me. "It sounds smarmy, but dogs want a family. They've been thrown out of one. I think they know it."

"I believe you," I said.

"Of all God's creatures, dogs are the ones most capable of gratitude and loyalty. Those poor little guys can't do it any more." He sighed. "Their chances are slim. I can't think about it," he said. "It'll ruin my fishing."

During the rest of the drive Steve appeared to do just that as we talked of other things, but I returned to Savannah and her sisters, not that I wanted to. Some lucky people seem to be able to put unwanted thoughts out of their minds; I could never do it. Renee and Big Girl were not born into the world like most people I know. They were dumped here, strays passing through the neighborhood. Like those dogs, they would be hard to rescue. This cold thought did nothing for them but it made me ease up on them, a relief for me. When I laid off condemning them like an ayatollah, I spent less time thinking about them and what happened in my living room. They would have bit me, but ultimately they were pitiful.

Meanwhile, Becky was merciless. Momentum had shifted her way. She would be able to block my shots for a long time. I joined her for hall duty after second period class the day I went back to work. The kids were loud that day, yelling and slamming lockers. After the silence of my house it was jarring, but I was glad to be back. Becky and I leaned our backs against the wall, shoulder to shoulder.

"I'm glad you're back. It's about time. I never knew anyone who took sick days so they could have an orgy." She asked me how I felt. I told her just to feel normal was excellent. I thanked her for helping me.

"If I hadn't been so weak I could have put up a fight."

"If you hadn't been so weak you would have begged that scrawny girl to move in with you."

She asked me who they were. She referred to them, then and later, as "your friends," and Renee as "your little ho girlfriend." I told her she was jealous but it was a feeble defense. Giving her the background story filled up the time between bells. When I joined her after third period she was able to say what she had been waiting to say.

"I always wanted to act like that when one of my students wouldn't put up a phone. It felt kinda good," she said, warming up to her punch line. She turned to go to her room. "By the way, coach, from what I could see that night, which was everything, you don't have what it takes to be a porn star. Hey, how was that chicken noodle soup?"

She kept it up till it got tedious, and then some.

You skip a couple of the traffic lights on Rogers Avenue if you use one-way B Street to get to downtown Fort Smith. Traffic is lighter on B and you don't have to pass decaying structures on Rogers which were once classic squeeze-in hamburger and barbecue joints, or the asphalt parking lot where Billie Garner's Supper Club was located. I'm too young to have gone in there more than once or twice at its sad end and I'm wistful about that, because the old guys still around say although it wasn't a fancy joint, you could listen to a jazz orchestra, hear good clarinetists, trumpeters and sax artists who dropped in, and watch dolled up gals jitterbug. They say guys in the pool room arguing over debts pulled guns on each other every once in a while to settle things but, unlike now, no one was ever stupid enough to pull the trigger, much less come back and shoot up the place.

The B Street route may not have had reminders of what is lost, but it had a troublesome connection for me. St. Boniface Church and the Rectory across the street are split by B, making it tough as I drove by to forget about my church non-attendance since my friends, as Becky called them, pushed their way into my house. It wasn't that I was still carrying a burden of trash from the incident with the girls. Becky had done an effective job of beating the resentment and shame out of me with her sense of humor, a technique probably not used too much in the counselor world. I wasn't even mad about the incident anymore. If Father Mario neglected to tell us that the unfortunate we are trying to help might stab us in the back, that was okay. Being taken advantage of is "part of the overhead," an activist friend once told me. It was okay, too, that Father Mario never warned us that a close up view of the downtrodden means you better brace yourself for a look at depressing, self-destructive behavior. My pal would say that's part of the overhead, too. Truth is, I was disgusted with God, not man.

One evening I zipped down B Street on my way to 906 Cigar Bar on Garrison Avenue for an Aroma De Cuba and a glass of John Jameson and Son whiskey, which I was starting to ritualize to the status of sacrament. Impulsively, at 18th, I hit the brakes and parked sharply at the curb in front of the church steps. Early to meet my friends, I turned the motor off and looked again at the martyr Boniface above the church doors, kneeling at the foot of a pagan oak. Boniface's killer raises his sword over the kneeling saint. I had studied that scene many times, trying to read the expressions. The religious ecstasy oozing out of St. Boniface is maybe a little corny and overdone, but the Germanic warrior is not expressive. He is not conflicted. Politely declining the saint's help is not his makeup. If his features convey anything, his say he relishes the prospect of killing the man who wants to save him.

The neighborhood was quiet. Chimney swifts were chittering overhead, the zig-zagging flock beginning its disorderly but flawless plunge into the chimney on the old school. Two Mexican families stood outside their pickup trucks beside the side entrance to the church, the parents chatting in low voices as their happy kids in their prim uniforms chased each other around the parking lot. The day was closing softly, settling a mood over the neighborhood so tranquil it seemed to slow time. Suddenly, an ultimatum from my subconscious arrived. It came as unexpectedly as a news alert. I could not go back in that building. It was startling, and simple. It arrived with force and was not welcome. I wanted it to go back to the depths, the realm of blind salamanders.

I knew its creator: there was no harmony between the gospel readings I listened to every Sunday and God's creatures getting dumped. How long the conviction would last was a mystery, but a cold certainty washed over me. Without fear, I realized I was as bitter toward God as Narisi is to the people who shove pitiful dogs out of vehicles on lonely roads. But, how could I turn my back on the source of priceless gifts?

There was a lot to leave behind. The doors to that old building had opened up for me art and music and a body of written works accumulated over centuries. Under the open-beamed ceiling I had been comforted and cleansed, strengthened and healed. It was there that I learned that I was deeply, natively flawed, and also that I am royalty, the son of a spiritual king. In its beneficial confinement I was forced to experiment with throwing off my selfishness to give me space to ponder forgiveness and gratitude. I had learned to say, formally, without question, that I had done wrong in what I had done and in what I had failed to do, when I wanted to say, "If I have …if I have…"

It was where I worked out grief and where I celebrated. A substance had rubbed off me there: the capacity to love more people and love them harder that I was capable of on my own. The peaceful spirits of my mom and her many kind, devout friends, fellow widows who outlived their husbands by decades and who became saintly, flowed through the walls to assure me and elevate me. I needed, desperately, for these things to stay with me, but a tether had snapped. I wasn't going back till something changed.

Edward Hendricks Wakefield

Edward Hendricks Wakefield, 74, died Wednesday, April 14, 2032 at his home in Fort Smith, AR, after a long battle with cancer. He was born in Aurora, Colorado on November 24, 1958.

He was a retired math teacher and coach. He loved golf, travel, and reading history. Ed was a member of The Ancient Order of Hibernians, the Noon Exchange Club, and was a volunteer official at Razorback track meets. He will be missed.

Ed was predeceased by his parents, Roy Wakefield and Polly Hendricks Wakefiled, and a sister, Wilda Mae Wakefield. He is survived by two sisters, Carol Widmer and husband Kurt of Portland, Oregon; Liz Craycroft and husband James of Estacada, Oregon; beloved nieces Allison Bobb and Megan Engel; and his caregiver during his illness, Mary Wakefield.

Funeral service will be Monday, April 19 at 10:30 at St. Boniface Church: 319 N. 19th, Fort Smith. There will be no visitation or graveside service. Memorials may be made to St. Boniface Church or Children's Emergency Shelter: 3015 S. 14th, Fort Smith, AR 72903.

About the Author

John Casey is a third generation teacher and the parent of a teacher. He is a kayaker and a hiker. Appreciation for stories, tales, quips, quotes and anecdotes is a family legacy.

About the Photographer

Mark Burnett played professional baseball until a backpacking trip to Europe opened his eyes to the connectivity in the world. He enjoys highlighting that connectivity, whether in wine & food, music & moments, or photography & art. His knowledge of wine pairings and alchemist's skill at concocting cocktails has made him a celebrated figure among his friends, including the author.

Both men are happy to report being in contented marriages. It is assumed that their wives feel the same way.

www.ingramcontent.com/pod-product-compliance
Lightning Source LLC
Chambersburg PA
CBHW070329120726
47909CB00008B/2651